WITCHY TROUBLE

Witchy Fingers 1

NIC SAINT

PUSS IN PRINT PUBLICATIONS

Witchy Trouble

Witchy Fingers 1

Edited by Chereese Graves

www.nicsaint.com

Give feedback on the book at:
info@nicsaint.com

facebook.com/nicsaintauthor
@nicsaintauthor

First Edition

Printed in the U.S.A

Chapter 1

*E*delie Flummox was snuffling in her sleep. It was what she did. Only now the snuffling was more pronounced than usual, and when finally she heaved the loudest snuffle of all and woke herself up in the process, she found that someone had dropped a pair of panties on her face, which were impeding her normal breathing pattern. She blinked, for she'd been dreaming of Colin Firth asking for her hand in marriage, then slowly allowed her eyes to drop to the panties and finally pick them up between thumb and forefinger, regarding them rather sternly. Scant light pierced the heavy drapes, but it was enough to determine the origin of the panties, which were pink and frilly.

"Estrella," she grumbled in an undertone. It took her a few seconds to gather herself sufficiently to swing first one, then a second leg from beneath the covers and locate her slippers, then another few seconds to heave herself up from the warm and comfy bed and, groaning, make her way to the door.

She loved sleeping and consequently hated being awakened while engaged in her favorite pastime. Judging by the nippiness in the air, giving her goosebumps, and the darkness suspended over the world like a pall, it was still the middle of the night. She was holding the panties out in front of her, suspended from her fingers, and proceeded across the landing, the ancient wooden floorboards creaking and groaning where she stepped, until she reached her sister's room. The triplets occupied adjoining rooms on the second floor of Safflower House, their ancestral home, so she didn't have far to go.

Edelie didn't bother knocking, but simply entered the room by pressing down the aged brass door handle. The door swung open with a creaking sound that would have scared anyone else. Edelie didn't even notice. She'd lived here for so long she was blissfully unaware of all the peculiar and wondrous sounds the house made. She flicked on the light, located Estrella, fast asleep, her head where her feet should have been and her feet on her pillow, and lifted the sheet, then deposited the panties on her sister's head.

"Brought you a present," she grumbled when Estrella tentatively opened her eyes and looked up questioningly. "Next time keep them in your drawer."

Estrella frowned as she surveyed the present. "Hey," she lamented sleepily, then yawned cavernously. "Those are mine!"

"I know they're yours. So what were they doing on my face just now?" Edelie asked, still peeved. She loved to sleep more than her sisters did, more than any human in existence probably, and was especially crazy about those sleep cycles that gave you the nice dreams of Colin Firth proposing marriage.

Estrella's pixie face quirked into a grimace, and she pushed her blond hair from her brow, blue eyes flashing. "Guess they didn't agree with my policy."

Edelie plunked her large frame down on the bed, her eyes hooded and her cherubic face pale as usual. Unlike her sister, her hair was a dark burgundy, now almost black in the dark. "What policy? What are you talking about?"

Estrella leaned up on one elbow. "Well, I've been trying to get my clothes to adhere to a more rigid schedule, see. You know how we spend so much time every morning trying to decide what to wear?"

"Sure," said Edelie after a pause. She never took any time trying to decide what to wear. She simply picked the first thing from the pile, usually a baggy black T-shirt and a pair of black jeans, her usual costume. But she did know both her sisters were a lot fussier than she was, especially Estrella.

"Well, I've been trying to train my clothes to present themselves according to a number of variables. Like the weather forecast, my work schedule, what Kim Kardashian was wearing the day before. The usual, you know. Like for instance if it's going to rain I need to wear a jacket, right?"

"Probably," Edelie muttered, already wishing she'd never come over.

"But if I have an audition I need my flashy stuff, right? And if Kim is into browns and ochers I need to take that into account as well, of course."

This time Edelie didn't even bother responding, and was eyeing the door wistfully. She should have just dropped those panties to the floor and gone back to sleep. Who cared about panties when you could have Colin instead?

Estrella was now sitting up in bed, her face animated and her hands gesticulating enthusiastically as she was getting fired up about this latest project of hers. "Well, I've managed to put all of that into a formula and create a spell that organizes my wardrobe accordingly. So..." She checked the items off on her fingers. "Rainy audition day with Kim ocher? Or sunny studio day with Kim orange? Or..." She was practically jumping up and down on the bed now, the mattress squeaking plaintively. "Rainy studio Kim blue? Overcast audition Kim purple? Chilly audiobook Kim sexy..."

As her sister droned on, Edelie wanted to point out that since Estrella was a petite blonde and Kim Kardashian voluptuous and dark-haired, it made no sense to try and copy the reality star's style, but knew it served no purpose. "So?" she now asked, absolutely not interested in Estrella's experiment.

Estrella threw up her hands. "So something must have gone wrong, for my clothes are now all over the house. They seem to think I've instructed them to assist you and Gran and Ernestine as well, forcing themselves upon everybody." She gave her a goofy grin. "I must have made a mistake in the spell somewhere. Where did you say you found my panties?"

"On my head."

Estrella nodded seriously. "They seem to think they're headwear, and that for some reason you need them to keep your head warm during the night."

"My head is fine without your panties, Strel, so just keep them in your closet, all right?" she muttered, walking to the door in her usual slouch.

"Sure thing, hon!" Estrella said, chipper as ever. "Though I might need your help to reverse the spell."

In response, she held up a hand and left the room. And when finally she was back in bed, she was surprised to find three more pairs of panties waiting for her, as well as two cashmere sweaters and a dozen pairs of socks. She sighed, deciding not to bother to return them. Five minutes later, she was sound asleep, her head now kept warm by what must be half the contents of Estrella's wardrobe. There was even a brassiere dangling from her ears.

She was unaware, therefore, of the window as it was gently being pushed open from the outside, nor of the dark figure that crawled into her room.

Clad in black from head to foot, a black stocking obscuring his features, the intruder deftly placed a sneakered foot on the floor, then a second one, and waited for a moment, listening intently to Edelie's soft snores. Then, certain that he hadn't disturbed her, he proceeded into the room, producing a small flashlight, and soon was traversing the floor and opening the door.

Chapter 2

*R*onny Mullarkey cursed under his breath. Safflower House had been pointed out to him by Marty, one of his colleagues, who held a day job working for an electric company and cased out promising houses. He'd told Ronny he would at the very least come away with a flatscreen TV, Blu-ray player and a couple of tablets and smartphones, along with some nice jewelry the owners of the place kept in a small safe. Placed behind the painting of some old crone and suspended over the fireplace, he simply couldn't miss it.

Four women lived here, Marty had told him. Three young women and a sweet old grandmother, all sure to be sound asleep at the stroke of midnight.

But what Marty hadn't told him was that the front door was impenetrable, and so was the backdoor, and that to gain access to the place he had to climb a tree, shimmy along a branch and get in through a window on the second floor. And as he made his way across the landing, the floorboards creaked and groaned so much he was afraid he would wake up the entire house well before he'd reached journey's end!

He crept down the stairs, leaning heavily on the balustrade, trying to keep the weight off his feet. For a cat burglar, he was on the plump side, his paunch having grown quite a bit these last few years. Once upon a time he'd been so light on his feet they called him the human fly. Now he was more like the human bumblebee. Still, he was experienced, and there was no one in the business who could open a safe as deftly and gracefully as he could, his fingers merely flickering over the dial. And he'd just reached the foot of the stairs, licking his lips as he shone his flashlight on a nice antique vase when there was a gentle cough behind him. And as he spun around, his flashlight first fell on a pair of slippered feet, then on a platinum blonde of imperial aspect who stood regarding him with an icy look in her pale blue eyes.

"Oh, Ronny, Ronny, Ronny," were the first words out of her mouth.

Starting violently, he demanded, "How do you know my name?!" Inadvertently, his hands reached up to his face, ascertaining he was still wearing his stocking, thereby obscuring his features and his identity. As it was, he was annoyed that a homeowner would invade his privacy like this.

"I'm going to give you two choices," the dame said without bothering to answer his question. "Either you walk out of here right now, and never come back, or I'm going to call the police and have you arrested. What will it be?"

Under different circumstances, Ronny would have gone for the first option, but something about this woman irked him. Perhaps it was the fact that she was so cool and collected in the face of a home invasion, or perhaps it was that she seemed to regard him with a blend of pity and disgust. So instead of meekly walking out, he grumbled, "What about option number three: I tie you up nice and tight, and relieve you of your possessions."

She tsk-tsked lightly. "Wrong answer, Ronny." Suddenly she

raised a hand and waved it in a meaningful manner. "You should know that boys who don't behave get punished in this house," she added, then muttered something under her breath that he didn't catch. The next moment he felt a stretching sensation on the top of his head, and when he touched his scalp, he discovered to his extreme dismay that two protuberances had appeared there, stretching the black stocking. They felt like... big, floppy ears!

"Aargh!" he cried, then repeated, "Aaaargh!" and finally "Aaaaaaargh!" just to drive his point home.

"Those will remain there until you apologize," the woman announced sternly. She was clad in a long housecoat, black with tiny silver stars, and her eyes were now shining as brightly as those stars. She was a classically handsome woman in her fifties and didn't look like a grandmother to him.

"I'm not apologizing!" he protested. "What are you, nuts?!"

She tsk-tsked again, shaking her head. Then she was waving that hand again, and suddenly he experienced the same stretching sensation, but this time near his bottom, and when his hand stole over, he discovered he'd sprouted a tail where no tail had ever been!

"Hey! What's going on?!"

"That one will disappear when you apologize not only to me but to the victims of the last five houses you burgled," she said. "And that," she added, pointing to his nose, "will go away once you've returned all the stolen goods you purloined from those five houses and compensate the victims in full."

He touched his nose in despair. It was growing and growing and now felt more like a pig's nose than his own more moderate copy!

"You crazy woman!" he began to screech, but found that something was wrong with his vocal cords, for all that came out was "Oink! Oink! Oink!"

"Look, we can do this all night," said the woman, "but I rather think you must be getting the point round about now. So apologize already, will you?"

She was right. He was ready to apologize. But all he managed was more of the same. "Oink! Oink! Oink! Oink! Oink!"

She smiled. "Very well. Apologies accepted, Ronny." And when he abruptly raced to the door, yanked it open and stormed out, she yelled after him, "And don't forget to reimburse your last five victims. And apologize!"

And as he hurried along the street, his tail between his legs, he vowed to give Marty a piece of his mind for sending him into that place unprepared. "Sweet old grandmother, my ass!" he lamented. "That woman is a witch!"

Chapter 3

*B*reakfast was already sizzling on the stove when Ernestine descended the stairs and strode into the kitchen. She wrinkled her nose in disdain when she caught a glimpse of the frying pan. Eggs and bacon and a lot of fat, no doubt.

"You do realize you're setting yourself up for heart failure," she told her grandmother, who was jauntily sprinkling some frittered onions into the pan.

"Just cooking up a hearty breakfast for my three girls," she replied.

Ernestine held up a hand. "Ugh. Not for me. I would like to keep the walls of my arteries unclogged for another few years, thank you very much."

"Suit yourself," said Gran, unperturbed.

Cassandra Beadsmore was a sturdily built woman, who'd become a mother at eighteen, a grandmother at thirty-six, and now was young enough to pass for the triplets' mother instead of their grandmother. Which was just as well, since she'd singlehandedly raised them after their parents had mysteriously expired when the girls were barely out of their diapers. And even though the three sisters were twenty and gainfully employed,

Cassandra still mothered over them and looked out for them like she'd always done. To them, she was their mother, for they hardly remembered their own.

Ernestine took a seat, unfolding the New York Times and pushing her glasses further up her nose. "Mh," she remarked with a glance at a small news item, "apparently a man was caught running around Brooklyn last night, ringing doorbells and returning stolen goods and apologizing. The police were called in, and when they questioned this Santa Claus, they found he was the one who stole the items in the first place, burgling houses all over Brooklyn, and promptly placed him under arrest." She looked up at Gran. "Weird. Why would a burglar have a sudden change of heart like that?" she asked, puzzled. "It makes no sense at all." She was a keen study of human behavior and had at one time even contemplated becoming a psychologist.

Gran shrugged. "Must be a loopy person," she opined primly. "Now what are you going to eat, young lady? You must eat something, you know."

Ernestine raised her chin, and took out a box of muesli, then dumped some in a bowl and added milk. "Something that won't destroy my body."

Gran eyed the bowl critically. "That's chicken feed, honey. Are you a chicken or a human?"

Just then, Estrella came gamboling into the kitchen. "Who's a chicken?" she asked as she took a good, long whiff of the eggs and bacon. "That smells yummy, Gran!" she caroled happily, and plunked down at the table, ready to devour the treat. Unlike her sister, she didn't seem to share the same concern for her arteries. Instead, she poured herself a cup of steaming black coffee and fished a bagel from the basket, Ernestine looking on in extreme distaste.

"How you can eat that..." she said with a shake of the head.

Ignoring her, Estrella announced, "I had the weirdest dream last night. My wardrobe had suddenly gone crazy on me and was stalking the house."

"That wasn't a dream," Edelie said from the door as she came pottering into the kitchen. "That actually happened." She fished a pair of socks from her collar and threw them at Estrella. "There's more where that came from," she added dryly, and plunked down at the table, looking extremely tired.

Of the three sisters, Edelie was the least energetic one, and that was an understatement. Ernestine was the prim and proper one, and Estrella the peppy one, always ready for a laugh. The three Flummox women, in other words, were as different from each other as any human beings could be, and sometimes they themselves wondered if they were actually sisters at all.

Even their physical appearance was quite different. Ernestine was dark-haired with a straight-laced personality that was reflected on her face, which was delicate and pale with a small nose and thin lips that habitually turned down into a frown. Edelie was red-haired, round-faced and green-eyed, with a noticeable cleft in her chin. And Estrella was blonde and petite, with cornflower blue eyes and cupid bow lips that were practically perpetually quirked up into a cheeky grin. Still, since they were sisters, they shared many traits as well: all three of them were honest and good-hearted, they hated injustice and underhandedness with a vengeance, and loved Cassandra Beadsmore almost more than life itself and would leap through fire for her.

Not that Gran couldn't take care of herself. She hadn't merely raised the Flummox triplets as her own, she'd kept them out of harm's way as well.

In fact the only reason Edelie, Estrella and Ernestine still lived at home was that they shared a trait with their grandmother that was very rare indeed: they were, in fact, witches, and as such vulnerable to the scrutiny of the outside world. By sticking together, they kept each other safe and allowed the rare magical forces they'd inherited from a long line of witches, going all the way back to Fallon Safflower, who'd built Safflower House in 1848, to grow and nurture in the safety of their ancestral home.

"So what are you guys up to today?" Estrella asked, dunking her bagel into her coffee and taking a big, savoring bite.

"I'm going to interview a client today," Ernestine announced primly.

"That's a first," Gran said, wiping her hands on a towel.

Ernestine was a legal secretary with ambitions to be a lawyer one day, and interviewing a client was indeed a first for her. Usually the law firm of Boodle, Jag, Lack & Noodle where she was employed awarded her more menial tasks, like typing up reports or doing research. "I'm going to have the preliminary talk," she explained. "The client is going through a very painful divorce at this moment, and wants to be informed about his options."

"So you're going to handle the divorce?" Estrella asked.

She pursed her lips. "Well, not me personally, of course. My job is to find out what I can and then report back to my boss, Mr. Boodle."

"Right," Estrella said, nodding intelligently. She was trying to take an interest, Ernestine knew, which was commendable. Edelie hadn't even bothered to pretend she was listening. But then not everyone found the law as exciting as she did. She loved how it made sense of the world, and how through the justice system society was made a safer and more civilized place.

"And you, honey? What are you up to today?" Gran had addressed Edelie, whose head had practically hit her plate. "Huh?" she asked, sitting up with a jerk. "Oh, I'm trying out something new. S'mores with vanilla ice."

Ernestine made a face, but Gran said, "That's just great, honey!" and shoveled a truckload of eggs on Edelie's plate, who eyed them sorrowfully.

Edelie had ambitions to be a chef but unfortunately, unlike her sisters, wasn't the scholarly type and had dropped out of school. Now she worked at the Brigham Shatwell store in Manhattan, part of a chain of coffeehouses larger than Starbucks, where she occasionally surprised her manager with her new inventions. Only last week she'd done something remarkable with chocolate mousse, gelatin, and eggnog, and the customers had loved it.

"And what about you, Estrella?" Gran asked. "What mischief are you up to today?"

"New radio commercial for Teppy," Estrella said, sounding a lot more excited than the work seemed to warrant, in Ernestine's humble opinion.

"Sounds... challenging," Gran said with a nod.

Estrella grinned. "You mean boring, right? But I love it, you guys! Teppy—whiter than white," she added in a singsongy voice.

Estrella had dreams of becoming a pop star and had entered more talent shows than anyone Ernestine knew. Unfortunately, she wasn't much of a singer and hadn't fooled the Simon Cowells of this world. She was perky and oozed zest and zeal but no talent to speak of. So now she worked as a voice-over artist. It wasn't her dream job, per se, but she seemed to like what she did and was getting quite good at it, too. She was now gunning for her own radio show, more specifically one of those 'Advice to the Lovelorn' ones.

When finally all three women had eaten their fill, Gran announced, "Just remember, you guys. No magic outside the house today, all right?"

"We know, Gran," the three sisters said with an eye roll.

"I'll keep repeating as long as you keep forgetting," Gran said pleasantly, but with a hint of steel. It was Gran's golden rule. Even though the girls were witches in their own right, that didn't mean they were competent witches. In fact, they were just about the worst witches in the history of the world, and when they were younger Gran often had to jump through hoops to undo the damage they'd done to their school friends or unsuspecting visitors.

So a new rule had been established, one that Gran insisted on to this day: they weren't allowed to practice magic outside of the house. The only person allowed to use magic was Gran herself, because at least when she cast a spell, no disaster ensued.

Ernestine caught sight of the kitchen clock and rose from the table so quickly she almost upset her empty bowl. "Gotta go!" she announced and quickly pressed a kiss to Gran's cheek. Today was a big day, and she couldn't be late!

Chapter 4

*R*onny checked his watch over and over again, intermittently drumming his fingers on the glass table. He adjusted his shirt—the only one he owned— then finger-combed his spiky hair and finally checked his watch again. He'd stolen it from an elderly couple on the Upper East Side last summer. According to the inscription, it was a retirement present for thirty years of faithful service as a fireman. He liked it. It had heft, something modern watches didn't have, made out of plastic as they invariably were.

He liked quality, and he appreciated real workmanship. He considered himself an artisan of the trade, a real craftsman, and was proud of the skill set he'd acquired. He had large, gray eyes and a broad face and a fleshy nose which gave him a rather squished aspect, perhaps because for the better part of his adult life Ronny had been wearing a black stocking over his head.

He'd stretched out his legs, crossing them at the ankles, and found himself studying the ceiling. It was off-white, like the rest of the place. He hated offices and he hated waiting so he was doubly annoyed for being here. But the guy had called him the minute he left the police station and told him he had a great job lined up. And since he was feeling testy after last night's fiasco, he'd decided a great job was what he needed to get out of his funk.

Not only had he been forced to return all of the stolen goods he'd purloined or make some other form of restitution—for he'd already fenced most of them—it hadn't taken those stunned homeowners long to call the cops on him, and now he was facing a nice long stretch in jail if the judge found him guilty of breaking his parole. The only reason he wasn't in jail right now was that they were full up with real criminals: the rapists and murderers and other bad apples. A petty criminal like him apparently could await sentencing from the luxury of his own home. Not that he minded. He didn't like to go to jail. If possible, he tried to avoid the place like the plague, and usually did a pretty good job at it, too. He hadn't seen the inside of a prison cell in months. Until that witch had turned him into a pig last night.

He still didn't understand what had happened, nor could he tell any of his friends. Who would believe him?! Heck, he didn't even believe it himself!

He looked up when a sonorous voice interrupted his thoughts.

"Mr. Mullarkey, I presume?"

He found himself gazing into the face of a very large, very formidable man. Not only was he built like a basketball player, but he had one of those elongated powerful faces that stood out. And then there were his eyes. Dark as obsidian and fixed on him with an intent stare that gave him the willies.

Instantly he sat up. "Yeah, that's right. You said you had a job for me?"

The man chuckled, a sound of metal grinding on metal. "I might indeed have a job for you, Mr. Mullarkey. If you're up for it, that is."

"Oh, I'm up for it," he said, and he wasn't lying. "If you want I'll steal The Donald's favorite hairpiece from Trump Tower itself."

"That won't be necessary," the man assured him, as he took a seat across from him. The entire setting felt like he was doing a job interview of a sort. Which was weird, for he'd never worked an honest day's work in his life.

"It is my understanding that you came into contact with Cassandra Beadsmore last night?" the man asked, folding his hands in front of him.

He frowned. "Cassandra who?"

"The house you broke into belongs to Cassandra Beadsmore. She's the woman who..." He grimaced. "... made slight alterations to your person."

He was staring at the man now, flabbergasted. How did he know?

"The tail?" the man asked, quirking an eyebrow. "The ears? The nose?"

Ronny gulped at the recollection. "How do you know?" he finally asked.

"I have ways of finding out things," the man simply said.

"Yeah, well, she did that to me," he finally said, actually happy to get that weird experience off his chest. "She gave me those ears and that tail and that nose and then told me that if I didn't apologize and right the wrongs I'd done that she would give me a lot more too."

The man shook his head commiseratingly. "What a terrible ordeal you went through, Mr. Mullarkey. What a terrible, terrible ordeal."

"You know it," he said, nodding vigorously. "She half scared me to death."

The man stared at him for a beat and seemed to measure him up. "What I'm going to propose is going to sound a little... strange to you."

"Nothing can be stranger than what happened last night, Mr..."

"Just call me Joshua."

"Well, Joshua, believe you me, some weird shit went down last night."

"I do believe you, Mr. Mullarkey, which is why I want you to return to Safflower House..."

"Huh? What?"

"... and apologize profusely to Cassandra Beadsmore."

He was shaking his head even as the other man was finishing his sentence. "I'm not going back there," he announced. "Never in my life."

"... and once you're there, and she has accepted your heartfelt apology, I want you to give her a small token of your appreciation," the man went on, taking no heed of Mullarkey's protestations. He produced a small pouch and placed it on the glass table in front of Ronny.

In spite of his objections, Ronny's curiosity was piqued. "What's that?"

"Open it," Joshua said, leaning back and adjusting his three-piece suit.

Ronny loosened the string and opened the pouch. He was surprised to find three gems inside. They looked like diamonds, only they were three different colors. One was yellow, the other blue and the third one was red.

"Are these diamonds?"

"You don't need to concern yourself with what they are exactly, Mr. Mullarkey," Joshua said in his rumbling baritone. "Simply hand them to Mrs. Beadsmore and tell her that this is your way of making amends."

He shrugged. "Why don't you give her these yourself?"

"I have my reasons. In exchange for your cooperation," he said, placing his hands together, "I'm willing to pay you one hundred thousand dollars."

"Done!" Ronny said, jerking up from his chair and stretching out his hand. For a hundred grand, he was willing to do anything, even to return to that horrible woman and relive the horror of slowly being turned into a pig.

Joshua smiled and shook his hand warmly. "It is certainly a pleasure doing business with you, Mr. Mullarkey."

"The pleasure is all mine," he said with a smirk. He then quickly pocketed the gemstones and eagerly searched around for a briefcase with his money.

"You'll get the money once you've delivered the stones," Joshua said.

He wasn't happy about it, but the man didn't look like the type who was ready to do some haggling, so he merely asked, "How will I get my money?"

Joshua grinned. "Don't worry, Ronny. I'll know where to find you."

It should have been an innocuous statement, but somehow it gave him the creeps. Just like everything about the guy gave him the creeps. But then beggars aren't choosers, so as he took his leave he thanked Joshua for this opportunity. Oddly enough, when he examined the stones later at his walk-up, he discovered they were cold to the touch. As cold as ice. Or death.

Chapter 5

*E*delie rode the subway morosely as it carried her and about five million other New Yorkers into Manhattan. She knew she should count herself lucky to have found a job at Brigham Shatwell, the hottest new chain of coffeehouses to hit the States, but frankly she abhorred the work. She wanted to be in her own kitchen creating recipes, like Julia Child, or be on TV like Nigella Lawson, or even running her own empire like Martha Stewart. She envisioned a future of cookbooks with her name on the cover, and cooking shows, and even her own magazine like Oprah. She could just see it now. And as she looked at her fellow commuters, she imagined people reading not the *Post* or the *Daily News*, but *E, The Edelie Magazine* instead.

In reality, she was in the business of preparing coffee in all flavors and sizes for a never-ending stream of customers on a daily basis. She didn't even particularly like coffee, and the only thing that provided a sparkle of joy was that Ginger allowed her to spend some of her time dreaming up new creations of her own. This was exceptional, for most of the stuff Brigham Shatwell carried was trucked in pre-baked and simply heated up.

She got off at her designated stop and climbed the stairs to the surface, where she was greeted by two bums seated on either side of the subway exit.

She dug into her pocket and came out with a dollar bill, which she promptly let flutter into the hands of the elderly African-American man who seemed to consider this subway station his home. According to the piece of cardboard he held up, his name was Julius, and he was 'grateful for all.'

He gave her a radiant smile, a single silver tooth glittering in the morning sun. "Thank you, ma'am," he said courteously. "May your day be blessed and your every touch be magical!"

She smiled back at him, his words giving her a tiny thrill of cheer.

And as she walked on, she wondered if magic was indeed her ticket out.

She'd tried before to use magic to further her goals, but it had always backfired on her. Like that time she'd decided to cook dinner for a dozen of Gran's guests, one of whom was a well-known food critic. She'd had the crazy idea that if only she could impress him with her cooking, he'd offer her a career on a platter. So she decided that her usual cookery wasn't enough, and had decided to use a little magic. There was no rule about using magic indoors, so she was well within her rights, right? She'd simply stood back and cast a few spells that had quickly turned the kitchen into a war zone.

Apparently the ingredients didn't respond to her spells as she hoped, and the end result was that the turkey she was supposed to baste had looked like it had gone through the Hulk transformation, green tinge and all, and that the petite potatoes had turned into steel balls sprouting tiny razor blades that would have sliced the critic's taste buds clean off instead of enticing them.

And then there was the soup, which had turned into a boiling bog of the most hideous smell, and the veggies, which had turned animated and were now stalking the kitchen in search of havoc to wreak. Gran had to intervene, and had quickly whipped up a replacement meal to save the evening.

The veggies had been lurking in corners for weeks, though, and so had the steel potatoes, launching themselves at guests with lethal intent.

The disaster had induced Gran to instigate a new rule: no more subjecting unsuspecting visitors to magic in any way, shape or form.

Even though the memory still rankled, Edelie wondered if perhaps she should give magical cooking another try. She was older and wiser, after all.

And it was then that she caught sight of a giant eagle soaring overhead, apparently keeping in step with her. She looked around to see if anyone else was noticing, but as usual New Yorkers appeared quite oblivious of the world around them, moving in packs as they crossed the streets and hurried along, chattering into their smartphones or checking their Facebook statuses.

She glanced up again, and frowned when she saw that the eagle had descended, now hovering only a dozen feet overhead. She could clearly see the majestic bird as it spread its mighty wings. And she was just wondering if she was seeing things, for no one else seemed to be looking up, when the bird swooped down and promptly made a dash for her backpack!

"Hey!" she yelled when the mighty ruler of the skies snatched her backpack and quickly absconded with the treasured item, ascending with powerful upward thrusts of its wings. "Hey! Give that back!" she cried as the eagle quickly moved higher and higher even as she stood watching.

Fuming now, she decided to throw caution to the wind and disobey Gran's silly rule. Desperate times called for desperate measures, after all, so she quickly cast about for a spell that would return a lost object. Gran had taught the spell to Ernestine when she kept misplacing her glasses, so Edelie was quite certain it would work on her backpack as well.

"*Tornari*, um, *oh!*" she muttered hesitantly, waving her hand the way Gran had shown her, making a pinching gesture with her thumb, index, and middle finger.

And probably it would have worked if only she hadn't faltered midway through the spell—or perhaps there was a problem with her intention, or the gesture itself, for instead of her backpack landing safely in her grasp, there was a massive whoosh! as suddenly she found that she'd taken flight herself, and was now high up in the sky, joining the eagle. A quick sideways glance told her that her arms had sprouted feathers and that she was now… flying!

Instead of a mighty eagle, however, she looked more like a plump pigeon.

Chapter 6

"*U*m, birdie!" she called out, the moment she'd recovered sufficiently from her surprise.

The proud eagle, however, didn't even deign the newcomer a glance.

"Hey, you!" she yelled, anger trumping fear. "Give me back my stuff!"

This time, the bird did look over, but if he was surprised that the woman he'd just robbed of her backpack had joined him, he didn't show it.

"What are *you* doing up here?" he merely asked, sounding rather blasé.

"I want my bag back," she told him, panting a little from the exertion.

"Oh, you mean this?" he asked, indicating the backpack he was still grasping firmly in his claws.

"That's my bag and you know it, you... bird!"

"Of course I know that this is your bag. Why else would I take it?"

She frowned, not comprehending. "Just hand it back already, will you?"

She was finding this flying thing a lot more taxing than she would have imagined, and her arms were getting tired really fast trying to keep up with the eagle. How birds did this, she didn't know. Lots of practice, probably.

The bird appeared to smile, or at least that's how she interpreted the slight change in the composition of his feathered face.

"There's something I need to tell you," he said, "and I figured the only way I could get your full attention was if I stole that bag of yours."

She stared at him. "You did this just to get my attention?"

"That's right. So listen up, Edelie Flummox, because this is important."

The nerve of the bird! "How did you know I'd come after you?"

The eagle actually rolled his eyes! "Puh-lease. With your poor grasp of the magical process? You were bound to make a mistake and end up here."

"Hey! I'll have you know my grasp of the magical process is impeccable!"

"Of course it is. Now listen up. Someone out there is coming after you."

"Yeah, you," she muttered.

"His name is Joshua and he's after your powers—such as they are."

Her fellow bird was swooping down, and she had the hardest time keeping up. "You're speaking in riddles, bird!" she yelled over the wind.

"First off, I'm not a bird. I just donned this guise to approach you. Secondly—and listen carefully because I will only say this once—Joshua can only be stopped if you take away his powers before he can take away yours."

"And how do I do that? You just told me I'm not much of a witch."

"That's why you need to team up with your sisters. Together you can take on Joshua. Alone? Not so much."

"And all this from a talking bird," she muttered.

"I'm telling you," the bird repeated slowly, "I'm not a bird."

"You look like a bird to me."

"Have you ever seen a bird talking? Or stealing backpacks?"

"Not really," she had to admit.

"I'm trying to help you here, so just pay attention already, will you?"

He was still swooping lower, and Edelie had the hardest time keeping up. "Hey! Bird!" she now panted. "My arms are killing me, so if you don't want me to splat down in the middle of Manhattan and make a mess, I suggest you get to the point."

"I told you already. Find Joshua before he finds you, and vanquish him."

"Vanquish." She actually laughed at that. "I don't *vanquish* people."

"You should. And he's not people."

"Look, bird," she began.

"Will you stop calling me bird!"

"What else can I call you?"

"Just call me Tavish. Tavish Mildew," he said, and then suddenly swept down and landed deftly on the top of the Empire State Building. Edelie, of course, missed her approach and shot right past the iconic building.

"Hey!" she cried as she zoomed past. "My backpack!"

"Safe landing!" Tavish shouted, and he was actually grinning!

Her arms were now too tired to carry her weight much longer, and she suddenly regretted having eaten such a big breakfast—

or having eaten big breakfasts for her entire life! She was going down and she knew it, the wind whipping her fuzzy face and the earth racing up to her at dizzying speed!

"Crap!" she yelped, trying to remember a spell—*any* spell—that would keep her from landing with a horrible splat. She quickly stammered the first spell that came to mind, and suddenly, even as she was swooping down, she found her limbs turning to rubber and her entire body morphing into a black rubber ball of outsized dimensions.

"Oh, no," she muttered just before impact, and then she was bouncing her way through early morning traffic. If being a bird was tough, being a rubber ball was perhaps even tougher. She was bouncing off cars, and fire hydrants and manhole covers, and off the tops of people's heads, and when finally she was starting to lose some of her bounce, some kid snatched her from midair and started playing with her, throwing her against the wall and deftly catching her. Finally, she'd had it. She was sick and tired and nauseous to a degree, so she whispered another spell, and lo and behold, suddenly found herself sitting next to Julius in front of the subway station!

The entire episode had exhausted her, so she simply sat there for a while, glad to feel the ground beneath her feet. So when suddenly the elderly homeless man turned to her and told her, "Find Joshua and vanquish him," she jerked up with a startled cry. And then she was hurrying away from him, only to stop when he yelled, "Hey! You're forgetting something, ma'am!"

It was her backpack, dangling from his fingers.

She approached him a little warily, trying to figure out if he was Tavish Mildew or if Tavish was merely using him to convey his message, and snatched her backpack from his hands, then hurried away again.

"Have a great day, Edelie!" Julius now caroled. "Full of magic and fun!"

"Fun," she grumbled, shaking her head. She hadn't had much fun at all!

Using magic was all well and good, but with her level of ineptness it was a miracle she hadn't killed anyone. Or herself, for that matter.

And as she outpaced a flock of New Yorkers, her phone rang, and when she picked it up, she was treated to the irate voice of her manager Ginger, asking her where she was. She was late. Again.

She jogged along and thought about what Tavish Mildew had told her. Who was this guy, anyway? And what was all this talk about Joshua coming after them? Who would ever come after three totally inept witches like them? She decided to put the whole thing out of her mind until tonight, when she could talk to Gran. Well, at least the part about the warning. She wouldn't tell her about turning herself into a bird or a bouncy ball, of course. As if it wasn't bad enough that Ginger was mad, she didn't need Gran mad as well.

And then she'd finally reached Brigham Shatwell, and burst inside, moving past a throng of irate customers, and weathered Ginger's angry looks as well as she could. And as she tied an apron in front of her, she popped a muffin into her mouth, remembering the one redeeming thing about this job: she could eat as much of the leftover pastry as she liked.

Chapter 7

*E*strella was straining her voice and still the producer wasn't satisfied, as he kept gesturing from the other side of the glass to sing higher. Higher! Higher!!! A manic man with Ray-Ban Aviators and a mane of blond hair that wouldn't have looked out of place in the eighties, Mike Hognose had been pushing her all morning, like one of those crazed workout trainers on TV.

But she couldn't possibly go any higher than this! Her voice, she meant to say, had its natural restrictions, and could only reach a certain pitch. She was recording a new commercial for Teppy, the well-known laundry detergent, and instead of the tried and true 'Washes whiter than white!' they'd gone for 'Try Teppy and make your laundry happy!'

And she'd been trying in vain to hit that high note at the end, belting out 'happy' like an opera diva, when it occurred to her that a little magic might do the trick. Producer Mike kept yelling at her, and she kept failing to hit that high note, so she quickly whispered one of the spells Gran had taught her.

It had the capacity to distort the human voice. Gran liked to use it to turn someone's voice into a pig's snort or a cow's moo or a parrot's squawk.

Gran loved it, and so did the three girls when they were little.

Couldn't the incantation work on her voice as well? Turning it into something that would make an opera star proud? Of course it would!

"," she muttered now, waving her hand just so.

"Okay, take it from the top!" Mike yelled. "And this time hit that high note! Hit. That. High. Note!" he screamed, pointing to the ceiling, as if that would induce her to sing higher, "or else we're gonna be here all day!"

"Oh, no, we won't," she murmured, and then launched into the jingle.

"Try Teppy and make your laundry happieeeeeeeeeeeeeeeeee!"

As she hit that last note, she gave it her all, belting it out with everything she had until the note seemed to take up every ounce of space in the small recording booth and then some. The high-pitched sound reverberated around the room and was so loud it was like a jet going through the sound barrier!

And as she stood panting, she opened her eyes, proud as heck. She'd nailed it! She just knew she had. And when she looked up, her hands still pressing her earphones to her ears, her face quite red now, she found Mike staring back at her, shock etched on his features. She smiled at him.

"And? Did I hit it?" she asked, her ears ringing from the sonic boom.

Only now did she notice that the thick pane of glass that divided the control room from the studio had somehow disappeared, and when she glanced down she saw tiny pieces of glass all over the floor and the mixing console. Glass shards were in Mike's hair and on his clothes and even falling from his lips, and it was obvious that by 'enhancing' her voice she had perhaps overdone things just a tad.

She gave Mike an apologetic smile and an "Oops!"

Ten minutes later she was walking to the bus stop, clutching her bag and thinking dark thoughts about the producer, who'd fired her on the spot. She didn't know what was worse: that Gran would be upset she'd practiced magic outside of the house, or that she'd lost her job even though she'd done exactly what they'd asked her to do. What did the guy expect? Nobody could hit that note without a little help. Well, perhaps Mariah Carey could. Though she kinda doubted Mariah would have destroyed the studio in the process.

She sighed as she rounded the corner on her way to the bus stop. And that's when she saw him. An African-American man dressed in black from head to foot stood eyeing her keenly. She blinked, only to find that he was gone. First he'd been standing there, watching her, and then he was gone!

She sighed again. Now, on top of everything else that had happened, she was starting to see things as well! Could this day get any worse?

She didn't have long to wait, for the bus almost instantly rumbled up to the curb, belching diesel fumes. And since it was only ten o'clock in the morning there weren't too many passengers, so she had the luxury of space. She took a seat near the back, wanting to give her thoughts free rein.

She was going to have to find another job, but with this latest incident, that might prove a little difficult. And then there was the fact that she didn't particularly like being a voice-over artist. She wanted to be a singer, not spend her days selling laundry detergent. She loved singing, even though honesty compelled her to admit she wasn't very talented. But wasn't there a way around that? There were so many popular singers who couldn't sing, so why couldn't she be like them? They used special equipment in the studio and a lip-sync machine on tour and no one was ever the wiser.

Or she could be a rap artist, writing her own stuff, and simply yelling her way through her songs. People loved that kind of stuff, didn't they?

"Excuse me but is this seat taken?"

She didn't even look up, but merely nodded her head. But when she caught sight of the black pants and the black shoes and the black socks, her gaze quickly traveled up to the black shirt and the black hat, and she recognized the man as the one who'd been checking her out before!

Suddenly horrified, she started to scoot away from him, but he silenced her concerns with a hushed, "I'm not going to harm you, Miss Flummox."

Her jaw dropped at this. "How do you know my name?"

He grinned, and she admired two rows of perfectly even white teeth. Hollywood, she instantly thought. Or perhaps a dentist?

"Neither," said the man, reading her mind as if she'd spoken the words out loud. "I'm here to help you, Estrella."

"Help me? Find a job, you mean?" was all she could think of to say.

He laughed, and it wasn't an unpleasant sound at all. More like a friendly rumble, and for some reason it sounded oddly familiar.

"Do I know you?" she asked therefore.

He eyed her keenly. "You might," he admitted. "Though last time we met you were so young you probably don't remember the occasion."

She watched him with perturbation, and suddenly blurted out, "Dad?"

He laughed even harder, and she saw why. The man was dark-skinned and she whiter than Teppy. Besides, her dad was dead, according to Gran.

"Not exactly, though I did know your father. And your mother."

This surprised her even more. "You—you knew my parents?"

He nodded. "Quite well, actually. But let's not get into all of that. I'm here to warn you. There's a man who calls himself Joshua out there who means you harm. His name isn't Joshua, of course. In fact he's not even human."

"What is he, then?" she asked, though the story sounded too fantastical.

"He's what you might call a representative of the Dark One, the force of evil that's hell bent on turning this world of ours into a rather nasty place."

"And this guy... is coming after me?"

"You and Ernestine and Edelie, in fact. And if you're not careful he will strip you and your sisters of your powers and destroy you in the process."

"Our... powers?"

"Yes, I know you think you don't have any powers, but you do."

She eyed him without comprehending. How did this guy know so much about her while she didn't know the first thing about him? It didn't seem fair.

"Well, it isn't, of course, and once this whole mess is cleared up, we'll all get together and shoot the breeze, but not now. Now you need to find Joshua before he finds you. Stop him before he destroys you, you understand?"

"But where is he? And what does he look like?"

"Just follow the signs, Estrella. And talk to your sisters. It will take all three of you to battle Joshua."

"But what about Gran? She's a much more capable... person than us."

He smiled a wistful smile. "I know she is, but this time she won't be any use to you. This is one you have to handle yourself."

"And why is that?"

He eyed her for a long time. "Because Joshua... *is* your grandmother."

And with these remarkable words, he suddenly vanished before her very eyes. She'd been leaning in to ask more questions, and now that he was gone, she practically fell into the next person, an elderly lady who looked worried.

"Are you all right, dear?" she asked in a reedy voice. "You were talking to yourself for a moment there, did you know that?"

"Yes—yes, I know. I'm sorry about that." She pushed at her blond bob. "Tough day at work."

"I understand, dear," said the woman with a merciful smile. "Don't you worry about that nasty boss of yours. You just give as good as you get, you hear?" And before Estrella could stop her, she launched into a long-winded story about how she'd been booted out of the company she'd started herself.

She tuned her out and thought back to what this strange man had said. Joshua *was* Gran. But how could he be Gran if he was after their powers? She didn't know, but it was imperative she talked to her sisters. Right now.

Chapter 8

*E*rnestine was grinning at the client and she knew it but couldn't stop herself. It was all the fault of that horrible spell she'd cast on herself!

The moment the client had walked into the conference room she'd known she was in big trouble. She'd been waiting for him, poised and composed, dressed in her best charcoal suit, her hair tied back in a tight bun and her black-rimmed glasses lending her the solemnity this interview demanded. And then she'd caught sight of him and she'd heaved an audible gasp.

The man reminded her so much of her favorite actor Hugh Laurie!

With his elongated face and his puppy dog eyes, he was the British actor's spitting image. She'd seen all the episodes of *House M.D.* several times, and Maybe Baby, of course, and everything else he'd ever been in, and had developed the kind of adulation that was perhaps more fitting for Estrella, not the more down-to-earth person she was.

But she simply couldn't help it. The man had charm and class and wit and was, above all, a world-class actor. When *House M.D.* had ended, she'd wept bitter tears, and had briefly contemplated casting a spell to force the network to keep the show on the air for perpetuity, or at least for as long as she lived. That Mr. Laurie would have reached a respectable age by then didn't bother her. He was, after all, a character actor, and didn't rely on good looks alone.

Though in her own humble opinion he was the most handsome man alive.

And now here he sat, this Hugh Laurie lookalike. For a moment she'd thought he was the man himself, but he'd given her a different name. Lyndon Bloom. But he talked with the same irresistible British accent, and had the same funny face, and when he smiled he dipped his head the same way, his lips quirking up. For all intents and purposes this was Hugh's identical twin.

So she'd quickly cast a spell to appear as irresistible to him as he was to her. Not merely because she suspected here sat her favorite actor of all time, but because he was a client. Her first client, in fact. And she wanted to make an impression he would never forget. Or neglect to mention to her boss.

So she'd been grinning at him and simply couldn't stop, even though he seemed to consider her attitude highly inappropriate in one who was supposed to represent his interests.

"So then she cheated on me with her first lover," he was saying, "and I didn't really think very much of it. These things happen, I mean to say."

"Very noble of you," she said, displaying her toothy grin.

"Yes, well, we'd only been married for a few short weeks at that time, and I figured she hadn't gotten the hang of the thing yet. Didn't fully grasp the rules of the old marriage game, if you know what I mean."

"Of course," she said awkwardly. Grinning, she found, made talking very difficult indeed. "Especially the rule that you shouldn't cheat on your spouse."

"Exactly! So when it happened again I was understandably upset."

"Understandably."

"And then when it happened a third time and a fourth..." He coughed, visibly embarrassed to spill these intimate details to a perfect stranger, especially one who couldn't stop grinning at him like a complete idiot.

"How many times would you say she cheated on you?" she asked, pen poised over her yellow legal pad. She'd been scribbling away incessantly, though mostly doodles featuring Hugh Laurie surrounded by hearts.

"Twenty-four times," he said, carefully patting his hair. "Over the course of a five-year marriage that makes for an average of, oh, about five lovers a year? Quite a record, I would imagine. Though of course I'm not an expert."

"And how did you find out about these... lovers?" she asked, cursing Mrs. Lyndon Bloom. Who would go and cheat on Dr. Gregory House!

"Well, actually she was the one who told me. Seemed quite proud of the fact. Made it a point that I met every lover in person. Of course she didn't introduce them to me as her lovers, but she would point out some random bloke at a reception or gallery opening, and then later would confide in me that she'd slept with the chappie. For some reason it seemed to excite her."

"So what induced you to remain married to this woman?"

"Well, I loved her, of course," he said. But then his composure faltered and he rubbed his face. "And then there's the fact that I'm a complete and utter ass! I probably should have divorced her from the first instance."

"Especially since she kept doing it over and over again," she pointed out.

"Well, there is that, of course." He shrugged. "Why did I stick around? Laziness? Cowardice? Fear of being alone? I should probably talk to a shrink about this, for there must be something seriously wrong with me."

"Oh, no!" she assured him. "There's nothing wrong with you, Mr. Bloom. Quite the contrary. You're absolutely perfect." When he frowned at this, she was quick to point out, "I mean, perfect for her. You tolerated her behavior."

"Well, I didn't tolerate it so much as tried to ignore it," he said, then leaned forward. "Look, um, Miss Flummox, I've been meaning to ask... Is there something wrong with your face? It seems to be stuck in the same mode, as it were."

"Oh, you mean this?" She pointed at her ridiculous smile. She couldn't tell him she'd cast a spell to appear attractive and it had gone horribly wrong. "Yes," she said after a pause. "There is something wrong with my face."

"You should really have that looked after," he said with a frown. "It's... I don't mean to be rude here, but it gives a fellow the wrong impression if you know what I mean. A lack of consideration for my, well, rather sensitive issues. If I didn't know any better I'd think you were simply laughing at me."

"Oh, no! I can assure you I'm not!"

He gestured at her. "See? You're doing it again. You're telling me one thing while your face is telling me the opposite. So please... stop doing that."

"I—I'll try," she said, and desperately cast about for a counter spell to render the effect of the first one null and void. She quickly whispered, "*Karismatractivus*," which she hoped would solve the issue, but instead of having the desired effect, it appeared to make things worse, for Bloom uttered a startled cry and jumped up from his chair. "Oh, dear Lord in heaven!"

"What is it?" she asked, perturbed.

He was holding up his hands in feeble defense. "Just... Don't look at me like that, please!" he cried.

She quickly glanced at the window and caught a glimpse of her reflection. Her face was contorted into such a malevolent grimace that it wouldn't have looked out of place on Hannibal Lecter's visage, ready to savor Mr. Bloom's liver with a side dish of fava beans and a glass of Chianti.

"Oh, I'm so sorry," she muttered, trying to fold her features into a less homicidal expression and failing miserably.

Lyndon Bloom was now backing away slowly, still holding up his hands as if to ward off evil. "I'm—I'm afraid I can't continue this interview," he stammered. "I'll, um, I'll get in touch with Mr. Boodle, shall I? Reschedule!"

And with a final horrified wail, he streaked from the conference room.

The moment he'd left, she buried her face in her hands. Oh, God. That had backfired to such a horrible extent! Then a soft cough sounded and she looked up, horrified to find that Spear Boodle was standing there, eyeing her a little uncertainly.

"Are you... feeling quite well, Ernestine? You look a little... weird."

"I'm... I just need a moment, sir," she said, avoiding his gaze.

"Yes, well, take all the time you need... to compose yourself," he said, and after another long moment, finally and mercifully left the room.

She sank into her chair. This was probably the end, she thought. Her big break and she'd blown it, just because she wanted to make a lasting impression. Well, she sure had impressed him. He'd probably never forget.

And she was trying to come up with another spell to break

the effect of the first two when a fruit fly started buzzing around her head. Annoyed, she waved it away, but it insisted on landing deftly on the tip of her nose.

For a moment, she peered at it, and was surprised to find it had a face!

She shrieked out her surprise and uttered a spell in the process. Instead of either returning her own face to its customary expression or removing the fly from her nose, she suddenly felt herself shrinking and turning about the size of the fly. Oh, God! What had she done now!

And it was then that she discovered it wasn't a fly at all, but a small human being, dressed in black from head to foot, and regarding her with an amused expression.

They were both perched on the table now, she sitting on her tush on her yellow legal pad, and he standing on the mahogany table, looking dapper.

"What in the hell did you do to your face?" he asked with a chuckle.

"And what did you do to me?!" she shot back, annoyed.

On top of everything else that had happened, she so didn't need this!

"I didn't do a thing. You did this," he pointed out. "I merely anticipated your capacity for casting terrible spells and acted accordingly." He wagged a reproachful finger. "Your grandmother won't be too happy about this, Ernestine Flummox. In fact it isn't too much to say she'll be furious."

"Who are you? And how do you know so much about me?" she demanded.

"Who I am doesn't really matter, Ernestine, but my message for you does. So listen to me very carefully. There's a man out there who's going to try and steal your powers—what little powers you possess—and you need to find him and stop him before he has a chance to do so. You and you sisters have to find this man and take his powers before he can do the same to you."

"What the heck are you talking about?"

"Just ask your sisters. They'll know," he said curtly.

Then, with another shake of the head and a chuckle, he simply vanished!

"Oh, for crying out loud!" she yelled. "Don't leave me like this!"

"Don't worry, Ernestine," the man's voice suddenly boomed around her. "Fortunately for you your spells lack staying power! Soon you'll be fine!"

And sure enough he was right. After another minute or so, Ernestine found herself growing back to her usual size, and when she glanced into the window, she saw that her expression was back to normal as well. Phew!

And then suddenly her phone started ringing off the hook, as both Estrella and Edelie apparently needed to have a word with her. Urgently!

Chapter 9

*C*assandra frowned when the doorbell rang. She had a keen sense of foresight, and this visit wasn't something she'd foreseen. But then, of course, there were always things that slipped past her vigilance. Like the fact that all three of her girls were out doing magic today, even though they knew very well they shouldn't. She hadn't seen that coming. Or the fact that Estrella would lose her job. She wasn't too worried about that, however, for she knew Estrella was clever and resourceful enough to land another. And what she also hadn't foreseen was that there were certain aspects of the triplets' day that seemed... blurred. Obstructed. As if they weren't letting her get the full picture of what was going on with them. But, as with Estrella, she didn't worry about that either, as the girls had a right to their privacy.

She'd been taking care of them for so long that sometimes she forgot they weren't children anymore but adults. Young women perfectly capable of taking care of themselves, even if they didn't always know it themselves.

She put down her garden shears and wiped her hands on her gardening apron, then set foot for the house. Her garden was her whole life, and whenever the weather permitted she was outside, pruning her gardenias or carefully submitting new and exciting species to the earth. Species she concocted in her own greenhouse, far away from the world's prying eyes.

She hung her apron on the hook behind the kitchen door, smoothed her clothes, patted her hair, and strode through the house and into the hallway. Through the rippled glass of the door she could see a person patiently awaiting her, and even before she opened the door, she knew who it was. She was pleased, actually, that he'd returned, his intentions obvious.

"Ronny," she said therefore the moment she opened the door. "It's so nice to see you again. And this time without the tools of your trade, no less."

The thief seemed surprised at this warm welcome. Whatever he'd been expecting, it most certainly wasn't this. But he quickly recovered, and gave her a lopsided grin. "I, um, I wanted to apologize about last night, Mrs..."

"Beadsmore," she said pleasantly, pressing his proffered hand. "Cassandra Beadsmore. Why don't you come in, Ronny?" she added as she stepped aside.

"Thanks," he muttered, still looking slightly ill at ease.

He wasn't all bad, she knew. Like many people he'd made a lot of bad choices, but with a little nudge he could be put on the right path. And she liked to think that perhaps last night had been exactly the nudge he needed.

She led the way into the parlor and bade him take a seat. He accepted hesitantly, his rather scruffy appearance quite out of sync with her own. He was wearing frayed jeans and a tattered old Giants sweatshirt. Cassandra, on the other hand, even though she'd been gardening, was looking spiffy, if she said so herself. She was dressed in her favorite pair of beige slacks today, along with a Louise Ferron blouse, accessorized with the earrings she always wore, the ones with the three hoops of platinum, representing her three girls.

The earrings appeared to fascinate Ronny, as his shifty eyes kept returning to them, his hands worrying his ratty beard as he did so. She wasn't surprised. To a professional thief like him the trinkets were quite enticing.

He appeared equally impressed with the parlor, which was one of her favorite rooms in the house. She'd had some help from Estrella when furnishing it, in bright and cheerful colors and a floral motif that extended throughout the entire house. The windows were stained glass but allowed a lot of light to stream in, and in the evenings the myriad of small lamps lent the room a cozy happy atmosphere that her frequent guests had all profusely complimented her on. Ronny, too, was looking around appreciatively.

"Nice place you got here, Mrs. Beadsmore."

"Thank you. Do you care for a cup of tea? Some homemade cookies?"

"Don't mind if I do." He seemed grateful for her courteousness. It probably didn't happen very often that a home he'd burglarized was opening its doors to him with such a display of hospitality, but then Cassandra believed in offering a person a second chance, and even a third and a fourth.

Moments later, she returned carrying a tray with a teapot, two cups and saucers, spoons and a plate of homemade chocolate chip and almond cookies.

"So, what brings you here, apart from apologies?" she asked as she poured two cups of chamomile tea.

"Well, I did what you told me to," he said, devouring a cookie whole and making appreciative sounds, "and apologized to all those people. And you were right. I don't understand how I could ever have done those horrible things. Breaking into those homes and taking what wasn't mine..." He eyed her with sincere contriteness. "Thanks to you I see the error of my ways now, Mrs. Beadsmore, and I want to make amends somehow. Put things right."

"Sometimes we need but a moment of reflection to know we're going down the wrong path," she pointed out as she took a dainty sip from her tea.

"Well, you were right. I traveled down the wrong path for far too long."

"And now you feel you're on the right track again, is that right?"

"Absolutely. After the lesson you taught me, Mrs. Beadsmore, there will be no more burgling houses for this guy." He laughed. "Not after that tail and that nose..." He faltered, giving her a furtive look of genuine trepidation.

"Don't worry, Ronny," she said, leaning forward and touching his knee reassuringly. "There won't be any repetition of what happened last night."

He laughed a little too loudly at that. "Phew. That's a load off my mind."

"Did you return the stolen items from the other homes like I told you to?"

"I did," he said, nodding. "Yes, ma'am, I certainly did. Even though they called the cops on me and had me arrested, I still paid them back in full."

"Yes, well, that was to be expected," she said mildly. Not everyone was as forgiving as she was, she meant to say. "I'm sure that if you display the same sense of remorse before the judge, he'll give you a second chance."

"Well, they didn't keep me locked up, so that's a good sign right there."

"If your case ever comes to court..." She eyed him with a

twinkle in her eye. "I could be a witness in your defense, Ronny. Would you like that?"

He looked up, greatly surprised. "Yeah. Oh, yeah, I would like that very much, Mrs. Beadsmore."

"Please, just call me Cassandra," she said, tapping his knee smartly. "You know what, Ronny? I think you and I are going to be very good friends."

He gave her a big grin. "That would be so great... Cassandra."

He fished in the pocket of his jeans and came out with a small purple velvet pouch of some kind and laid it on the side table between them.

She eyed it with rising curiosity. Somehow there was something off about the scene, though she couldn't put her finger on it. "What's that, Ronny?"

"This," he said softly, "is a small token of my appreciation. Just to show you how I feel about what you did to me last night. And to say sorry for trying to burgle your place." Then, without awaiting her response, he opened the pouch. Three stones rolled onto the table, startling Cassandra. They were yellow, blue and red stones, and she knew them very well indeed.

"What—what are you doing?" she asked, suddenly feeling faint.

He was eyeing her intently now. "Like I said, Cassandra, these are a present to you. And my way of paying you back for turning me into a pig."

Her hands were trembling as they reached up to her face, which was flushed. It was hot in here. Too hot, and her heart was beating way too fast. The stones were already exerting their power over her, and her mind had turned blank, her powers fading quickly. She had to remove herself from their influence. So she jerked up from the chair and staggered to the door.

"Oh, don't leave now, Cassandra," Ronny taunted. "Let's shoot the breeze some more, shall we? Good friends like us? Let's talk about my rehabilitation. Or, better yet, about those three girls of yours. Estrella, Ernestine, and Edelie, right?" He laughed, a nasty, mocking sound.

Cassandra never reached the door, for even before she'd put one foot in front of the other, she fell to the floor, hitting her head against the corner of the ornate cabinet that held pictures of her three granddaughters. Three picture frames fell down as she hit her head, dropping down on top of her.

Ronny was staring at her with interest, eyes wide and mouth curled into a wicked grin. He was licking his lips as he rose from his seat and watched with relish as Cassandra struggled to get up. But the stones quickly morphed into three hoops as strong as steel and tightened themselves around her, pinning her arms to her body and preventing her from moving even an inch.

"That's what you get for trying to turn Ronny Mullarkey into a pig," Ronny said softly as he stood over her. "A little taste of your own medicine."

Her eyes fluttered closed then, and soon she knew no more...

Chapter 10

The three sisters were seated in their favorite spot at Brigham Shatwell, Edelie having managed to induce Ginger to give her a short coffee break. Estrella and Ernestine had shown up within seconds of each other, and they now sat ensconced in the corner, the coffeehouse buzzing with coffee lovers.

Edelie waited until the others were settled in before dropping her voice to a low murmur to share her tale of the bird and rubber ball incident.

"He said his name was Tavish Mildew, and some bad man called Joshua is going to try to take away our powers if we don't get to him first!"

"I'll bet it's the same guy I met!" Estrella broke in, and regaled them with the story of how she met this man dressed in black from head to foot on the bus. "And he told me the same thing," she concluded breathlessly, "about Joshua! And he also told me he used to know our parents!"

"I met him, too!" Ernestine gasped. "He was a fruit fly but then he wasn't, and he told me this weird story about this Joshua person coming after us!"

After the threesome finished telling the stories of their weird and outrageous mornings, they shared meaningful looks. They didn't need much more to figure out that what was going on was extremely sinister to a degree.

"This... Tavish Mildew guy, what did he look like?" Edelie asked, and when both Ernestine and Estrella gave the exact same description, it was obvious they'd been approached by the same person, either in the guise of an eagle, a fruit fly or, as in Estrella's case, as the actual man himself.

"And he said he knew our parents?" Edelie asked.

Estrella bit her lip. "He said he did, but that I wouldn't remember him. He did look familiar, though. Maybe I recognized him from an old picture?"

"Let's go through Gran's picture albums," Ernestine suggested.

"Good idea," Edelie agreed. Even as engrossed as she was in the conversation, she kept an eye on Ginger. She couldn't take too long on her coffee break or there would be hell to pay, especially after arriving late.

"Or why don't we simply ask Gran?" Estrella said. "She must know him."

"Listen, you guys," Edelie now said, "I can't get out of here for a bit, or at least not until my shift ends. Maybe you can go home now and talk to Gran?"

"I had the same idea. It's just that..." Ernestine hesitated.

"You don't have to tell her about Hugh Laurie," Estrella assured her.

"Yeah, I wouldn't tell her about any of that if I were you," Edelie chimed in. "Just like I'm not going to mention turning myself into a fat pigeon."

The three sisters laughed. By now they'd broken so many rules it was hard to keep track.

"Tavish did say Gran wouldn't be any use to us," Estrella reminded them.

"He didn't mention that to me," Edelie said.

"Or to me," Ernestine added.

Estrella frowned as she tried to remember the man's exact words. "He said Gran can't help us because..." Her eyes widened. "Gran *is* Joshua."

"What?!" Ernestine cried, startling two men who looked like hedge fund managers, almost inducing them to spill coffee on their power suits.

"That's impossible," Edelie hissed. "How can Gran be an evil person?"

"Yes, she would never hurt us, or take our powers," Ernestine said.

"Well, she would like to take our powers sometimes," Edelie amended, "especially after the kind of morning we all had."

Ernestine shook her head. "That's different."

And it was different, of course. Edelie, too, couldn't imagine Gran ever doing anything against her three girls.

"She wouldn't even want to take away our powers," said Estrella. "Not really, I mean. She just wants us to be better witches. Not to abuse our powers or accidentally hurt people or create a mess like we usually do."

"Yes, all she's ever wanted is to turn us into better witches," Ernestine agreed. "So she can't be Joshua. You must have misheard, Estrella."

"I don't think so," Estrella said, shaking her head.

Ernestine pursed her lips. She'd had enough of this idle talk. "We'll talk to Gran and let her figure it out. She's the most competent witch we know."

"She's the *only* witch we know," Edelie muttered.

"And she'll be able to help us figure out what's going on."

"We don't even know if we can trust Tavish Mildew," Estrella pointed out. "For all we know he could be bad news, and Joshua doesn't even exist."

"Could be," Ernestine allowed.

"I did get the impression he was for real," Edelie said hesitantly, then caught Ginger's wave and sighed. "You guys, I have to get back to work. Talk to Gran and let me know what she says, all right?" And as she hurried away, she added, "Oh, and don't mention—"

"The 'incidents'?" Estrella smiled. "Don't worry, hon, we won't."

Edelie didn't like this. She wanted to be there when they talked to Gran. She wanted to see the look on their grandmother's face when she listened carefully. The look that said, 'I don't want you to worry about a thing. I know all about Tavish and Joshua. I've got their number.' And the smile that indicated, 'I love you guys and whatever you do, I'll always be there for you.' For deep down inside she knew that Gran was aware of what they'd been up to. She always was. And as she took her place behind the counter and took an order of Mocha Frappuccino with Cream and Chocolate Sprinkles, she watched her sisters leave and returned their wave.

Somehow she had a feeling that Tavish Mildew hadn't been lying, and that something very bad was about to happen. Something very bad indeed.

Chapter 11

*E*strella shared her sister's sentiments. She had a gnawing sensation in the pit of her stomach that told her things weren't on the up and up, and it had nothing to do with the fact she'd lost her job or that Ernestine had scared a client half to death. No, for some reason she was feeling anxious and sad at the same time, something that rarely happened to happy, peppy Estrella.

Twenty minutes after leaving Edelie, they stepped off the bus and hurried from the bus stop on the corner of Nightingale Street to their house. Ernestine hadn't stopped talking about Lyndon Bloom and how his wife had treated him horribly, and about the look Spear Boodle had given her when he saw her with that terrible expression on her face.

Estrella didn't care one iota about Lyndon Bloom or Spear Boodle or anyone else for that matter. All she cared about was talking to Gran and putting this whole weird episode behind them as soon as possible.

Finally, she caught a glimpse of Safflower House as it rose up behind their neighbor's conifers. All the houses on Nightingale Street had the luxury of small patches of front yards, and most people had turned them into miniature oases of greenery and floral delight. The moment she caught sight of Gran's forsythias, she felt a sudden peace and calm soothe her anxiety. Whatever the Tavishes and Joshuas of this world might be up to, they were no match for Cassandra Beadsmore, she knew.

The windows of Safflower House were stained glass, depicting colorful scenes of courtships and births—Fallon Safflower had been a midwife—and of course flowers in full bloom. Flowers were Gran's passion. She'd worked at a flower shop when she was young, and when the owner retired had taken over the store and had turned it into a small franchise of very popular flower shops called *Flor et Bloom*. When she sold the franchise to a national chain, it had given her the opportunity to retire young and devote the rest of her life to creating new flower species—and to raising three hell-raising young witches. Her flowers had won her many prizes and carried the names she'd given them. They were as much her babies as the triplets were.

Finally, they arrived at the house and hurried up the stone steps to the front door. Estrella inserted her key anxiously. The moment the door swung open, she called out, "Gran? Gran! We're home!"

The sense of foreboding that had held her in its grip throughout the journey home suddenly returned in full force, and she simply knew something terrible had happened to Gran.

There was no response, and as she glanced into the parlor, she saw to her surprise that a tray with cups and saucers was placed on the side table, along with a plate of cookies. She hurried over, and saw that the cup was half empty, a cookie half eaten, but when she looked around, she found no one there. She placed her hand on the teapot. Still warm. Then she caught sight of a small purple pouch. She picked it up. It was empty. She gripped it to her chest, fear puckering up her brow. "Gran," she murmured. "Where are you?"

Just then, Ernestine stepped in. "No sign of her," she said with a frown.

"Did you look in the garden?"

"And the greenhouse. She's not here, Strel."

Estrella pointed to the cups and saucers. "That tea is still warm."

"What's that pouch doing there?"

"No idea."

"Looks like something that would hold a gem," she muttered.

Estrella shook her head. "Something happened to Gran, Stien!"

"You don't know that. All we know is that she was here, had tea with a guest, and left. She could be next door with Renée for all we know."

Renée Reive was their next door neighbor and a good friend of Gran's.

Estrella nodded. "So let's try her cell." She took out her phone and tried Gran's number. The telltale sound of little tinkly bells had them gasping in surprise. The sound came from somewhere in the parlor! Ernestine was quick to drop down on all fours and search beneath the cabinet that stood next to the door and carried pictures of the three girls. She suddenly cried, "Got it!" And as she fished the phone from beneath the cabinet, she muttered grimly, "Must have fallen."

And as the two sisters' gazes locked, Estrella was the first to suggest, "Let's call the police. Something happened to Gran."

And for once in her life, Ernestine immediately agreed with her.

Chapter 12

*I*nspector Samuel Barkley was a big man. Tall and imposing, his mere presence told people not to mess with him. As a member of New York's finest, he'd worked his way up through the many departments that made up the NYPD and was very proud to be a homicide detective and a damn good one at that. He wasn't merely tall, he was also broad and muscular, built along the lines of a linebacker, and his square face, anvil jaw and piercing blue eyes spelled trouble to the bad guys that crossed his path.

He arrived ten minutes after Ernestine had put in the 911 call, his partner Pierre Farrier in tow. Ernestine had told the dispatcher her grandmother had been the victim of foul play and had given her to understand a murder had taken place at Safflower House.

It was enough to put Sam Barkley on high alert and arrive in record time.

Since Estrella Flummox had indicated her grandmother had been murdered, he'd decided to step on it. He didn't believe in wasting time. The sooner a murder case was underway, the sooner it was solved was his personal experience. It was with extreme disappointment, therefore, that when finally he arrived, he found no dead body waiting for him in the parlor.

He gave the tallest of the two sisters a dark frown. She was a dark-haired beauty with black-rimmed glasses. A real looker—not that that mattered. She seemed to be the one taking the lead and was therefore the one subjected to his opening question. "So where's the body?"

The woman gave him a rather nasty stare. "There is no body. Gran is missing, not dead."

"Missing person, huh?" he grumbled. "I'm a homicide detective, lady."

"We believe our grandmother was abducted," the woman said primly.

"And you're basing this on... what, exactly?" he challenged. The woman—according to the file one Ernestine Flummox—had folded her arms across her chest and was watching him with less warmth than a dead fish.

"Based on the fact that she isn't here, that none of her friends have seen her, nor any of the neighbors—yes, we checked. And that we found her phone under that cabinet where it must have fallen when she was attacked."

"Attacked, huh? By whom?"

Ernestine pointed to two cups and saucers on the side table. "She was entertaining a guest. My guess is that this guest must have attacked her."

He sighed. Civilians. You had to hand it to them, their petty little minds never stopped working overtime. He blamed it on all those cop shows. It got people all hot and bothered about the smallest little thing. They saw a tea cup and a cell phone and immediately assumed the worst.

"Look, lady, I'm pretty sure your dear old Granny will turn up any moment now," he said. "Where does she usually hang out?"

"She doesn't 'hang out,' Inspector."

"Detective."

"She's usually home, and when she's not she leaves us a note."

"She does now, does she? And every single time, unfailingly, huh?"

"She has for the last twenty years," Ernestine said icily. "So I don't see why she would divert from that routine now, all of a sudden, unless, of course, something happened to her. Something like an abduction. Or worse."

He eyed the cabinet. "You're telling me her phone was under there?"

"It was."

He went down on hands and knees and inspected the piece of sturdy furniture. No dust. That was a first. Whoever this Cassandra Beadsmore was, she was a clean freak. And that's when he saw it. Smudges of crimson, and when he looked a little closer... a few strands of hair.

"C'mere," he grunted to Pierre, a smallish man with a salt-and-pepper mustache of which he was very proud. He pointed to the hair and the spot of crimson. "Check this out, will you?"

Ernestine and Estrella watched the exchange with worry etched on their features. So the moment he stood, Estrella asked, "What did you find?"

"Nothing to worry about," he said with a grunt. "Just some blood and hair. Could be anybody's." Estrella let rip a piercing wail that went through marrow and bone. "Could be anybody's!" he repeated. "Do you have a dog?"

"No," said Ernestine coldly.

"Cat?"

"Our grandmother doesn't like cats or dogs. They mess up her flowers."

"Weird," he said, glancing back at the blood and the hair. In his estimation it was fresh. So maybe there was something to the women's story after all. Then he directed his attention to the side table and saw the pouch. "What's that?" he asked.

"Something Gran's guest left," Estrella said. "We don't know what it is."

He pursed his lips, then told Pierre to bag the pouch, the teacups, and the saucers. "And while you're at it, bag the cookies too." They looked yummy.

"So what's next?" Ernestine asked when he strode from the room.

"What's next is that I'll get in touch with missing persons."

"But she's not missing," she pointed out. "There's blood on the cabinet from when she fell, and her phone was found under there. She was taken."

"For all we know she might have tripped, and this visitor took her to the hospital," he countered.

"Without giving us a call or leaving us a note? Never!"

"Might be. Stranger things have happened."

"Not to us."

And he could readily believe it. She looked like the type who had a really good handle on things. A tight grip. Too tight, perhaps, judging from that thought wrinkle dividing her brow.

"Look, lady, I'll ask around, all right? Call the hospitals and see if she hasn't been admitted somewhere. Meanwhile, stick around and pick up your phone. I'm sure your granny will be home any minute now, a nice big bandage on her head. Old ladies fall down all the time," he explained.

"She's not old. She's only fifty-six."

"Ah," he said, indicating that to him fifty-six *was* old. He walked to the door. "And don't forget to call it in when she turns up, all right?"

"She won't... turn up," Ernestine said, her voice quaking slightly.

"I'll bet you she will," he said, then touched his nose. "I've got a hunch."

And lo and behold, even as he spoke the words the doorbell jangled, and when he jerked it open, dear old granny stood on the mat, looking a little the worse for wear, a nice clean white bandage on her head... and supported by a guy Sam knew very well indeed. A guy with a big smile on his face.

"Ronny Mullarkey!" he barked. "What the hell are you doing here?!"

"Inspector Barkley," Ronny said, his smile faltering slightly.

"Detective. Don't tell me that after last night you've suddenly decided to become Good Samaritan as well as Robin Hood!"

"I—I just wanted to help Cassandra—Mrs. Beadsmore. She took a bad fall and, I, um, I took her to the hospital just in case."

"I'm fine now, though," the old woman croaked when she caught sight of Ernestine and Estrella. "Oh, my dears!" she cried and then the whole thing turned into a hugfest and Sam muttered, "Ugh," and looked away in disgust. There were even tears involved, so he muttered "Ugh" again.

He gave Ronny a long, nasty look. "I've got my eye on you, Ronny."

"I—I've changed my ways, Inspector."

"Detective! I don't believe you. Guys like you don't change their ways."

"Oh, but Ronny has indeed changed his ways," the old crone now piped up. "In fact, he's become quite a dear friend of mine, isn't that right, Ronny?"

"I'm honored to call Cassandra my friend," Ronny said, a little flustered.

"Ugh," Sam repeated and strode from the house. There were three things that sickened him to the core: puppies, teary reunions, and remorseful crooks. So he beckoned his partner. "Let's go, Pierre. I'm so done with this place."

"What about the evidence, Sam?" Pierre asked, hurrying up.

"Bring it along. We'll file it under the G of Gigantic Waste of Time," he grumbled and walked out after a final frosty glance at Ernestine. She returned his glance and added some frostiness of her own. Shaking his head he walked down the stone steps. "Last time I ever set foot in that house," he grumbled. "Place gives me the creeps." And he didn't know whether it was the house or the inhabitants, but when he looked up, he distinctly felt a chill settle in his bones. And, like his nose, Sam's bones were rarely wrong.

Chapter 13

*E*delie got the call shortly after three. Gran was fine, Estrella said. She'd fallen and hit her head, but she was fine. A very nice young man had been there to help her. He'd taken her to the hospital and then brought her home.

"And did you ask her about Joshua and Tavish?" she asked.

There was a pause, then Estrella admitted, "We haven't had a chance to ask her yet. She's... she's still feeling a little under the weather, and we don't want to bother her with anything that might upset her."

"Of course," Edelie muttered, then sagged a little. Her shift was almost over, but all through the afternoon she'd done nothing but worry about what Tavish Mildew had told them. "So when will you talk to her?" she now asked, chewing her fingernails. It was a habit she'd been trying to break for years.

"I don't know. Let's wait until she's feeling a little better, shall we?"

"And what about this Ronny guy? Who is he?"

"I don't know," Estrella admitted. "Gran said they met a little while ago, and he just happened to be at the house when she took that nasty tumble."

"Mh."

"Mh what?"

"Sounds like a very unlikely story," she said. Most of Gran's friends were middle-aged ladies just like herself. She didn't think there was any young man amongst her circle of friends, and now on the day she entertained this young man at her house she took this bad fall? So she repeated, "Mh."

"Enough with the mh-ing already," Estrella said with a laugh. "We should be thankful he was there. She could have been lying there for hours."

"What kind of person is he?"

"Well..." Estrella hesitated. "He seems... nice. A little... scruffy?"

Edelie snorted. It was just like Estrella to judge a person by their appearance. "I'm going to be another hour, and then I'm coming home," she said. She wanted to take a good look at this Ronny guy herself.

"Oh, he left already," said Estrella. "In fact, he seemed quite happy to go."

"Mh," Edelie repeated.

"Oh, stop it, Edie. He's perfectly all right. Otherwise Gran would never have said he was her dear, dear, *dear* friend."

Edelie could hear the eye roll. "She said that, did she?"

"More than once, so stop worrying. Tomorrow, when she's rested and has her strength back, we'll sit down with her, and discuss this Joshua thing."

After she hung up, Edelie found that the minutes ticked by so slowly she figured someone must have messed with the clock. Finally, when she simply couldn't take it anymore, she briefly considered making time go a little faster. Trouble was, she didn't know the spell to do that, so she decided not to even go there.

She'd done enough damage for one day, and magic wasn't going to help her cope with her tedious job any more than it had this morning.

Finally Ginger flipped around the closed sign, locked the door, and Edelie started cleaning up, readying the place for another day. Half an hour later, she waved goodbye to her boss and was on her way back to the subway station. She passed Julius again, but if the old man recognized her, he didn't give any indication. Even after she asked him if the name Tavish Mildew sounded familiar, he shook his head. "Uh-uh."

"Or Joshua?"

"Uh-uh," he repeated, then tapped his sign. "Grateful for all!" he caroled happily, and she gave him a smile and dropped a dollar note into his hands.

"God bless!" he said. "May you have a wonderful and magical night!"

She held up her hand as she descended the stairs. "I hope not!" she yelled back. As eventful as her day had been, she hoped that her evening would be a lot less so. She'd had just about all the excitement she could muster.

Chapter 14

*E*strella lay belly down on her bed, watching a rerun of *Keeping up with the Kardashians*. She didn't remember this particular episode and was always happy to catch some new little tidbit about her favorite family. In her humble opinion, Kim should become the next American president. She was sure she would turn that stuffy old White House into something hip and cool, and wouldn't her selfies from the Oval Office rock the nation? And what about Kanye as First Husband? Now that would be something really novel. And Kris could be Vice President, and the girls could all be Cabinet members!

She giggled and reached into her bucket of popcorn again.

Because Gran wasn't fully recovered yet and was now resting in her room, the girls had to make do, dinner-wise. So they'd ordered pizza, and for dessert Estrella had brought out her favorite acquisition: the popcorn maker.

Her door flew open, and a harried-looking Edelie dragged herself in, her face a dark mask of worry as usual. "Have you seen my tape recorder, Strel?"

Without looking up, Estrella asked, "What is a tape recorder?"

"It's that thing Gran gave me last week, remember? She found it at a thrift shop." She stared at her feet. "You, um, record stuff, and play it back."

"So why don't you just use an app?" she asked, wondering why Edelie kept bothering with that old crap.

"I *like* the tape recorder," Edelie said stubbornly. "It has class and elegance and an ageless beauty..." She sighed. "You wouldn't understand."

"Yeah, well, if you want to go all eighties on me, be my guest. Personally? I prefer to stay ahead of the times, not lag behind three decades."

Edelie smoldered a little, then seemed to drop her craving for decrepit old technology and plunked down on the bed. "How did Gran seem to you?"

"Fine, I guess. Just a little bump on the head. Nothing to worry about."

"Didn't she seem..." She hesitated. "... a little weird?"

Estrella frowned. This was her favorite part of the show, where Kim modeled her latest outfit. "Huh?" she asked. "Weird? What do you mean?"

"I don't know," said Edelie in a low voice. "She had a weird look in her eyes. I caught her staring at me, and it gave me the chills for some reason."

"What weird look?"

"As if she wanted to... eat me or something?"

Estrella laughed. "Probably just the pills, honey. They gave her some painkillers at the hospital. Against the headache?"

"Which is another thing that's so weird. This is Gran we're talking about. The super witch? When is the last time you saw her taking any pills?"

Estrella frowned. "Um... like, never?"

"That's right. Gran never takes any medication because she

can always heal herself with a spell. So why didn't she do that this time? Why pills?"

"I guess she wanted to try something new?" she suggested a little lamely.

"And why did she fall in the first place? Gran never falls. She's never been sick," she said, checking off on her fingers. "She's never taken any medication, and she definitely never trips or falls. She never, *ever* bumps her head. She's a witch, Estrella. Things like that simply don't happen to her."

"They happen to us," Estrella pointed out. "Remember how you used to trip up all the time? Especially when you were in your bell-bottom phase?"

"Yes, but we're the worst witches in the world," Edelie pointed out. "Gran is the very best."

"Huh. Haven't thought about that, actually."

"Well, I have, and I swear, Strel, when I came home and caught Gran staring at me like that? It gave me the creeps. She looked... really mean."

"That's not possible. Gran doesn't have a mean bone in her body."

"Well, I'm telling you that she has now," Edelie insisted stubbornly.

"Like I said," said Estrella, "she was out of it. Woozy from those painkillers." She gave her sister a mock punch on the thigh. "Just you wait and see. Tomorrow she'll be her old self again, cooking up a storm for breakfast, and trying to force Ernestine to start eating meat again."

Edelie grinned. "As if that will ever work."

"Well, you have to hand it to her, she doesn't give up without a fight."

At the age of fifteen Ernestine had suddenly decided she was going to be vegetarian, much to Gran's horror, and hadn't eaten a single piece of meat since. And Gran hadn't given up hope that one day she'd reintroduce her to the world of the carnivores. Not that she would ever succeed, Estrella reckoned. Ernestine was just about as stubborn as Gran herself. When those two butted heads, there was no telling who would win.

Edelie watched the Kardashians for all of five seconds, then rolled her eyes and was off to her own room again, leaving Estrella to enjoy her favorite show in peace. But as she was once again devoting her full attention to the adventures of what in her mind was America's first family, she thought back to her sister's words. Why hadn't Gran healed herself? And what was more, why had Gran hurt herself in the first place? Edie was right. For as long as she could remember, nothing bad had ever happened to her, so why now?

The reunion had been heartfelt, and Gran had seemed like her old self again, but had she? She'd been so happy to have her grandmother back that she hadn't really paid attention. The only thing she'd found strange was the presence of Ronny there, who apparently was something of a crook if that Detective Barkley was to be believed. And he wouldn't lie about that.

Then she decided not to dwell on this stuff. This was Edie again, of course. She always saw the worst in people and circumstances. Even in heaven, Edelie would find a fly in her rice pudding. That was just how she was. No, Gran was fine, and tomorrow they'd ask about this Joshua guy, and Gran would fix him like she'd fixed everything else for the past twenty years.

Chapter 15

*S*am Barkley took a bite from the chocolate chip cookie and nodded appreciatively. Whatever else he might think about Cassandra Beadsmore, she could definitely bake. He was staring at his computer, where he'd just finished typing up a report on the serial killer he'd been tracking for a while now. The guy had already left a long trail of bodies in his wake, and the latest one had just been fished out of the Hudson a couple of days ago. He always used the same MO: the victims were all young women, walking alone along the street, and they were all choked to death with some type of garrote that didn't leave a single trace, then dumped somewhere out of sight. They'd dubbed the perp the invisible choker, as no one had been able to determine how exactly the victims were strangled. The whole thing was a big mystery.

He stared at the cups and saucers in the plastic baggie placed on the edge of his desk. Pierre had dumped it there, and he frowned as he took in the small purple pouch that was lumped in with the rest of the stuff. It had obviously been used to transport jewelry of some kind. Which reminded him of something. If Ronny had indeed been the old woman's guest, it stood to reason that the pouch belonged to him, but why would a known thief like him visit old ladies and gift them jewelry? Usually he was the one to lift that stuff.

He quickly brought up the report on Ronny's latest arrest. The guy must have been high on something. Arrested while in the process of giving back stolen items to five homeowners, and reimbursing them in full. The first homeowner they'd interviewed had made a very weird claim. He said Ronny had been dressed up as if going to some fancy dress party: sporting pig's ears, a pig's nose and a tail, and even his speech had been garbled, sounding more like 'Oink oink oink.' The moment he'd handed them back their laptop, however, his voice had been restored to normal, and he'd told them, a little wild-eyed, that he'd been coerced into this by some crazy old witch!

Sam leaned back and frowned. Ronny himself had said nothing about an old witch or the fact that he'd been dressed up like a pig. He stared at the purple pouch again, then drew the plastic baggie within reach and opened it carefully, taking out the pouch. He turned it over in his hands, then unfastened the strap and peered inside. Nothing. The thing was empty.

He studied it some more, feeling the material under his fingers. It was expensive, he figured. Not something Ronny would have in his possession unless he'd stolen it somewhere. He tried to picture the scenario. Ronny had been visiting houses to return stolen goods and said he'd been forced into this by someone. An old witch. And next day he was visiting Cassandra Beadsmore, handing her a pouch of jewelry. The lady had fallen, bumped her head against the cabinet and taken to the hospital. It was all very fishy.

Then he heaved a loud grumble and dumped the pouch back into the plastic evidence baggie. Whatever Ronny was up to, it wasn't his concern. He'd spent enough time arresting the guy back in the day when he was still handling anti-crime. Now he had bigger and more dangerous fish to fry. Fish that abducted women, killed them and dumped them in the Hudson. Though Ronny Mullarkey was a nasty piece of work, at least he didn't go around killing people, so there was that to be said for the annoying creep.

He pushed the baggie away until it landed on Pierre's desk, then slapped a Post-it on it: 'Return to owner.' That was as far as his involvement went.

Chapter 16

*E*rnestine was lying in bed, staring up at the ceiling. All thought of Hugh Laurie had left her mind, and now all she could think about, for some strange reason, was Detective Sam Barkley. She didn't know why, for Barkley was absolutely not her type. Furthermore, he was a bully and hadn't been helpful when they called him in. Quite the contrary. If it were up to Barkley, Gran could have remained gone, and he wouldn't have lifted a finger to find her.

Still, there was something about the guy, something that reminded her of... of whom, exactly? Actually, she didn't know, for she'd never met a man like him before, a fact which fascinated her. He was fascinating to her because he was a novelty. A species of man she'd never met before. And she'd met men in all shapes and sizes, both in her personal and her professional life. She grinned as she thought back to Lyndon Bloom. Poor guy. She'd really scared the living daylights out of him, hadn't she? Perhaps he'd even change law firms on account of her. Well, suited him right. A man who allowed his wife to cheat on him no less than twenty-four times deserved a little scare. If someone had cheated on her even once, she'd have sent him packing.

And it was then that she caught sight of a curious object. A small spot on the ceiling, next to the Chinese lantern she'd once hung up there. The spot seemed kaleidoscopic in design, as if consisting of many different colors, and at first she thought it was a bug of some kind, a big fat fly. But even as she watched, it grew bigger and more colorful still, and finally was as big as a small TV screen, right there on her ceiling. And as she watched, unable to look away, she saw that it was a replay of the scenes that had occurred today.

She saw herself being reduced to a tiny spec, and then Tavish Mildew hove into view, telling her to track down and stop Joshua before it was too late. She groaned at the recollection. With all the things that had happened with Gran, she'd forgotten about the urgency with which the mysterious man had delivered his message, and she was reminded of the stories of her two sisters, who'd had the same experience. She watched as the small screen faded into nothingness again, and figured it was merely a projection of her own imagination, reminding her of the message she'd been given.

Tomorrow morning they would talk to Gran, she vowed, and find out what was going on. She was certain she would have heard of both this Joshua and Tavish and would be able to tell them what was going on.

And as her eyes drooped shut, the last image that appeared before her mind's eye was that of Sam Barkley, barking at her as seemed to be his habit. But then his grumpy features suddenly morphed into a much more endearing arrangement, just like Dr. House could be extremely gruff and grumpy one moment and charming and charismatic the next. For some reason she thought Detective Sam Barkley was actually a very interesting man indeed.

Then she drifted off to sleep, and all thought of the Sam Barkleys of this world were quickly forgotten. In her dream she was a small fruit fly, being chased by a man carrying bug spray, but as she tried to escape him, she got caught up in a strip of flypaper, and no matter how hard she struggled and fought, it was to no avail. She was caught and would die here. And with her last breath, she cried out, "Detective Barkley! Sam! Please help me!"

But all Sam did in her dream was grunt, "Ugh," and turn away.

Chapter 17

*M*orning arrived bright and early, and Edelie awoke with a groan. She didn't do bright and early. She much preferred to stay up half the night and sleep in. But she'd tried that, and the result was that she'd fallen asleep in the middle of pouring a customer a Double Latte Macchiato and had spilled the hot beverage all over herself. So nowadays she tried to be more like a normal person: early to bed, early to rise—however weird that was for her.

So she dragged herself out of the bed, fished one of Estrella's socks from her person—the same spell still at work, apparently— and slouched from the room, dragging a towel behind her. She was probably the last one up, but she didn't mind. At least she'd have the bathroom to herself, and didn't have to suffer the indignation of her sisters pounding on the door and telling her to hurry up.

She hated hurrying up almost as much as she hated bright and early.

When she arrived at the bathroom, she was surprised to find the door locked. After a tentative knock, a croaky voice announced, "Be right out!"

Her jaw dropped a little. "Gran? Is that you?"

"You bet it's me! Who else would it be? George frickin' Clooney?"

She stared at the closed door for a moment, wondering if she was still dreaming. Gran never got up this late. She rose with the chickens—not that there were any chickens in this part of Brooklyn—and was the last one to turn in at night. Finally, she felt compelled to ask, "Are you all right?"

"Never better!" Gran yelled. "Top of the world!"

"Yes, well, that's great," she muttered, and stood there for a moment, wondering what to do. She needed to take a shower, or else she'd be late for work, and knowing Ginger, she just might take her job away this time.

"Um, Gran?" she asked, therefore. "Are you going to be in there long?"

In response, the door suddenly opened to a crack, and she tentatively put her finger against it and pushed it open further. What she saw startled her. Her grandmother was... waxing her legs!

"What are you doing?!" she gasped.

The woman looked up, and Edelie was even more surprised to find that a cigarette was dangling from her lips. She took a long drag, then croaked, "What does it look like I'm doing? Did you know this hurts like hell?" She took a good grip on a strip and yanked it off, yammering "Owowowowow! How you girls manage to do this without a little magic, I don't know!"

Without a little magic? "So why don't you use magic, Gran?"

"Don't feel like it. Wanted to try it the old-fashioned way for a change."

Edelie stared at her grandmother's hair. It had taken on a strange color. A sort of blueish, greenish, pukeish tinge. "Have you been dying your hair?"

"Like it? It's called Danube Blue. Picked it up when I got back from the hospital yesterday. Ronny says it's all the rage these days."

"What does Ronny know about hair? Is he a hairdresser or something?"

Gran laughed a raucous laugh. "A hairdresser! That's hilarious! He's a thief, honey. A burglar, in fact. Specializes in cracking safes and stuff."

"A thief! But... how can he be your friend?"

"Don't you be hard on Ronny!" Gran admonished her. "He's a great guy."

This was getting weirder and weirder. "How do you even know him?"

"Met him the day before yesterday while he was trying to burgle the house," muttered Gran. "Taught him a lesson, didn't I? Turned him into a pig. Look, I think I'll stick with the one leg for now, this hurts too damn much."

Edelie stared at her grandmother, aghast. She *never* used this kind of language. "Your face!" she cried, only now taking a good look at Gran's face. "What did you do to your face?!" It was mottled, covered in red spots.

"Yeah, I used one of them face masks. Suppose I bought the wrong one?" She gave herself a quick glance in the mirror. "Yeah, guess I did." Then she shrugged. "Oh, well. Can't have it all, can you? Rich *and* beautiful?" She laughed again, then stepped into the shower and started undressing. "Do you mind, honey?" she asked, but Edelie had already left the bathroom, the sight of her naked grandmother not something she was willing to endure on an empty stomach.

And she was still clutching at her head when a shrill sound pierced the morning air. It was coming from downstairs. The smoke alarm!

Hurrying down the stairs in her black undies, she arrived in the kitchen just in time to see Estrella coughing and waving a kitchen towel at a pot on the stove, black smoke billowing up in thick, acrid clouds.

"What's going on?!" she cried, rushing over to open a window.

Estrella glanced over with eyes red from the smoke, coughing a little. "Gran told me to prepare breakfast! I've never done it before!"

That was true enough. Estrella might know everything about style, but she was a lousy cook.

"But why didn't she ask me? I'm supposed to be the cook around here!"

"I guess it didn't occur to her," said Estrella.

Edelie quickly moved over to her sister, bumping her out of the way, took out two oven mitts, grasped the smoking pot and hurried outside. Through the kitchen door she went, placing the pot on the stone terrace floor.

"What is that stuff?" she asked as she stared into the pot. All she could see were two black strips of something that might have been food once.

"Bacon," Estrella said. "I guess it didn't come out too well."

"You have to *bake* bacon, hon," she said. "And to bake something you need a pan, not a pot. You use this pot for cooking stuff, not for baking."

"Oh," said Estrella, chewing her bottom lip. "Good to know. Where *is* Gran, by the way? She disappeared after putting me in charge of breakfast."

"Upstairs, shaving one leg and ruining her face."

Estrella cocked an eyebrow. "She's acting a little weird this morning, huh?"

"A *little* weird? Try *extremely* weird," a voice announced behind them.

Ernestine had joined them on the terrace, and the three sisters now stood around the still smoking pot. Both Edelie and Estrella stared at their sister.

"Stien! What happened to your hair?!" Estrella cried.

It was as if a rat had taken huge bites from Ernestine's hair, turning it into something from *The Walking Dead*.

"I woke up when I felt something tugging at my head," she said, sounding a little subdued, her hand stealing up to touch her ruined hair. "It was Gran. She asked if I remembered the good old times when she used to cut our hair. I said there were never any good old times when she cut our hair, only good old times when she magicked our hair and made it look super-duper. But by the time I finally managed to make her stop, the damage was already done."

"Looks like that hit on the head did more harm than we thought," Edelie grunted.

"A lot more," Estrella confirmed.

"She's forgotten how to do magic!" Ernestine exclaimed.

"Who's forgotten how to do magic?" Gran croaked from the kitchen door. She was dressed in a ratty old housecoat, flapping around her half-shaven legs, a cigarette dangling from her lips, her hair the same ratty mess as Ernestine's, and a very weird color too, her face still mottled and swollen.

"Gran," said Ernestine carefully, "shouldn't you be in bed?"

"I'm fine," she said, waving a hand. "I feel like a million bucks!" Then she grinned, her eyes widening. "Hey, you know what we should do? We should go to the mall. Haven't been there in ages! Catch a movie, just the four of us. How about that, huh?! A day out with the girls!"

"Gran, I have to work," Edelie pointed out.

"So do I," Ernestine chimed in.

"Yeah, and I have to *find* work," Estrella added.

"Work?" asked Gran, taking a long drag from her cigarette, puckering her face into a frown. "Why work when you can have a ton of fun instead?"

The trio stared at their grandmother. This was not the gran they knew!

"Um, Gran?" Edelie asked. "Don't you want to lie down a bit?"

"Yes," Ernestine agreed. "You don't look too good. Why don't you take a load off your feet while I call a doctor, huh?"

"Doctor?! What doctor?!" Gran grumbled. "I don't need a frickin' doctor! I'm telling you guys; I'm on top of the world! Never felt better in my life. Now let's have some fun, shall we?" She pointed to Estrella. "You first. I want you to fix my hair for me, hon. Go on," she goaded when Estrella hesitated. "Cast a nice little spell that will fix my hair right up, will you?"

Estrella cast about for the right spell for a moment and finally seemed to have found it. "*Koifferato,*" she muttered without conviction.

"Louder!" Gran yelled. "And put some energy into the thing, will you?!"

A little louder, this time, Estrella repeated, "*Koifferato,*" and waved her hands about helplessly. The three sisters watched as Gran's hair started moving this way and that, then finally flopped down into some kind of blue pudding, piled high on top of her head. It looked even worse than before.

Gran patted her hair and grinned. "Thanks, hon. Feels great. Now you," she said, pointing at Edelie. "I want you to magic us up a nice breakfast."

Edelie gulped. "You want me to use magic... to fix us breakfast?"

"Sure! What else is magic for, huh?"

"But you always said I *shouldn't* use magic in the kitchen. Not since that time I practically destroyed the house."

"That was a long time ago," Gran croaked. "I'm sure you'll do fine this time. Now get cracking. I'm starving! And you," she said, gesturing at Ernestine, "I want you to fix the garden. Turn it into something presentable."

"Fix the garden? I don't understand," Ernestine said.

Gran waved an arm at the garden. "Look at this mess!" she yelled. She was pointing at the rose bushes, which were in bloom and looked gorgeous, like a feast of color and scent. "I want you to turn the place into a nice patio so we can host some decent parties around here. And back there," she added, pointing to the flower beds, "I want you to put a nice big pool. And add in a Jacuzzi, will you? Just put it where that ugly garden house is."

"But, Gran!" the three women yelled. "You love your flower garden!"

"Not anymore I don't," she said. "I'm sick and tired of messing about, digging in the earth like a frickin' worm. I want this garden to be something I can show off to my friends, not some sort of Amazon rainforest!" Finally, she gave the pretty little greenhouse a long, lingering look and a grin crept up her face. "And that," she said, pointing to the greenhouse, "has got to go."

"Gran!" cried Ernestine. "You don't mean that!"

"Sure I do." She thought for a moment. "Let's turn it into a garage. I've got my eye on a few nice muscle cars, and I need some place to store them."

And as Gran returned indoors, the three sisters were left staring at each other, horror displayed on their features. Gran was out of control, that look said, and she was quickly turning Safflower House into the House of Horror!

Chapter 18

*S*elena Bloom née Carter was walking along Arena Street, returning from an appointment at this cute little new nail salon she'd wanted to try out, and wondered where that persistent clickety-clack was coming from. The sound had been echoing in her ears for the past ten minutes, from the moment she'd left the salon, en route to the parking garage. She'd already checked her shoes, but the clickety-clack definitely didn't originate from her brand-new Jessica Simpsons. She'd stopped to look around, but the street was pretty much deserted, only a middle-aged lady walking a few feet behind her on the other side of the street. Figuring she was just being paranoid, she walked on.

Tossing her blond hair, she tried not to frown, because that would only lead to wrinkles, and at the age of thirty-six she had to protect the collagen in her skin like a lioness protects her cubs. She was on Botox, of course—had been for over a decade—along with every new revolutionary cream promising eternal youth, but still her pores were widening, and minor blemishes had started to appear on her face, especially around her eyes. Her latest worry was her bust, where extensive tanning was starting to show in the form of cleavage wrinkles. Very unflattering. She'd been using silicone pads at night to smooth out the skin and prevent sagging, and even injections with hyaluronic acid to plump up the skin, and saw a noticeable difference.

In spite of the fact she'd sworn never to frown again, she did so now, thinking about her latest dating disaster. She met Brandon—if that was even his real name—at Ruby Rourke's party last week, where she'd been celebrating her divorce. Lyndon, her soon-to-be ex-husband, was lawyering up, but her own lawyer, a woman who'd handled several celebrity divorces and had written the book on the subject—literally—said she had nothing to worry about. She foresaw a settlement to the tune of several million, enough to continue living the life she'd grown accustomed to as Mrs. Lyndon Bloom.

Brandon had told her he was a lawyer himself. Tall, dark and handsome, like all the men she'd dated throughout her marriage to that hapless sap Lyndon, he'd impressed her with stories about his Jag, his Manhattan condo, and his million-dollar trust fund. But when she'd called the law firm where he was supposedly a partner, they'd never even heard of the guy! He'd made up the whole story! And to think she'd invited the moron back to her place!

She'd instantly tried his cell, but the number didn't even exist! She'd been duped, and it irked her to no end. *She* was usually the hunter, *not* the prey.

There! It was that clickety-clack again, and this time it sounded a lot closer, as if someone was stalking her. She whirled around but all she could see was the middle-aged lady, now walking behind her, and she looked as unsuspicious and harmless as could be. Her eyes dropped to the women's feet. She was wearing high heels, she saw, and she almost laughed. All this paranoia for some dowdy old Carol Brady lookalike with heels. What a joke!

She gave the frumpy housewife a cold look and walked on.

She was passing a graffiti-sprayed wooden fence, put there to hide one of Brooklyn's eyesores: an abandoned construction site. She briefly glanced through a gap in the fence, and wrinkled her nose in disdain when she saw the maze of concrete pillars and girders rising up from a gigantic pit in the ground, twisted pieces of rusted rebar lending it an H. R. Giger feel.

She didn't notice, therefore, that the woman was fingering her ring finger intently, her eyes focused on the back of Selena's head. The ring, a gold band with a nice yellow diamond, was sparkling prettily in the New York sunshine. Just then, the stone popped from the ring and morphed into a small hoop that slowly drifted in the direction of Selena, spinning gently in midair.

With a soft crackle, it slung itself around her neck, and the effect was like a sudden heat around Selena's throat, and her hands instantly moved up to try to relieve the burning sensation. But instead, tension started building, pressing into the soft tissue of her throat, and before long she realized she couldn't breathe! She whirled around to cry for help, but the woman simply stood staring at her, eyes wide in obvious delight. And those eyes, she now saw, were the blackest black she'd ever seen.

She was being dragged toward the gap in the fence, and then she was squeezed through, tension around her neck still building, and then she was hurled over the edge, her terrified screams cut off by the murderous device choking the life right out of her.

Mercifully, Selena passed out even before she hit the bottom of the pit.

Chapter 19

*S*am got the call as he walked out of the Manhattan branch of Brigham Shatwell empty-handed. The skinny woman behind the counter looked harried, working her way through a long line of customers. Apparently, they were a man or a woman short, for the queue was crazy, even for a Brigham Shatwell. So he walked, cursing under his breath, and just then his phone rang. He picked it up with a gruff, "Yah."

"Sam, better get over to Brooklyn. The body of a woman was found..." The dispatcher hesitated before continuing, "It's Lyndon Bloom's wife."

"Oh, Christ," he muttered, putting his phone away and hurrying over to his car, where Pierre sat waiting patiently.

His partner looked up, his face falling when he saw that Sam wasn't carrying any gifts in the form of Brigham Shatwell coffee or donuts.

"Sorry, the line is too long, and we can't afford to wait," he grunted as he crawled behind the wheel. "We've got ourselves another homicide, buddy. Lyndon Bloom's wife."

"Oh, crap," Pierre said, looking distinctly unhappy. Whether he was unhappy about having to start his day without the best coffee and donuts in town or that one of New York's premier financiers had just lost his wife was hard to say. Probably the former, Sam thought as he put the car in gear, switched on the bubble and stomped on the accelerator, the Ford Crown Vic screeching away from the curb. Pierre had a sweet tooth and liked his donut of a morning. In fact, it was rare not to see him munching on something.

"Where?" Pierre finally asked, when his donut mourning period was over.

"Arena Street. Happened just now."

And as the car sped on, Sam thought he caught a glimpse of a beggar who stood eyeing him curiously from the sidewalk. He grinned as Sam zoomed past, a single silver tooth in his mouth. Sam held up his hand in greeting, and the bum returned the gesture, visibly pleased. Perhaps the guy liked cops?

They arrived at the scene and found the place already crawling with cops, putting up police tape to cordon off the area. He haphazardly parked the vehicle and joined the throng, Pierre close on his heels. And as he ducked under the police tape, he saw a familiar face. It was coroner Angela Jacobs.

He nodded a greeting to the stony-faced woman. "Fancy seeing you here, Jacobs."

"Fancy that, Barkley," she returned, unmoved.

Either the petite dark-haired woman was one of those anomalies who didn't possess facial muscles, or she simply didn't like to use them. Whatever the case, she had but one expression, and it wasn't a very friendly one.

He followed Jacobs as she made her away along the fence, then crawled through an opening. Sam had a little trouble negotiating the gap, as he was a great deal taller and bigger than the fine-boned coroner, but he finally managed, and so did Pierre.

The moment they'd stepped behind the fence, it was as if they'd entered a different and uglier world. The construction site was a dump, with a half-constructed edifice crumbling into a pile of concrete rot and rust, and a deep pit where the foundation was supposed to be. And down in that pit the body of a smartly dressed woman lay, face upward.

"Talk to me, Jacobs. What's the verdict?"

Angela shrugged. "Preliminary findings would suggest she was strangled with some kind of garrote. Not an iron wire or cord, though. Something smooth that doesn't leave a trace and extends all the way around the neck."

He shared a look of concern with Pierre. It was the invisible choker all right.

"And when did this happen?"

"In the last hour or so."

Sam looked up, surprised. "She was discovered so quickly?"

"A bum who likes to call this place home was just returning to put away some stuff when he happened upon her. He was so kind to call it in."

"Very nice of him," Sam thought as his mind flashed back to the silver-toothed vagrant he'd seen earlier. No connection to this case, of course.

"I'll file a complete report once I've got her back at the lab."

"Thanks. Appreciate it, Jacobs," he muttered, then slowly picked his way down to the bottom of the construction pit, along several plateaus. He stared down at the body, lying in a puddle of sludge. "What a waste," he muttered.

Pierre seemed to concur. "She was really pretty, wasn't she?"

"Yeah, she was," he agreed, kneeling down next to the body. He studied her earrings. One was still attached to her ear, while the other had seemingly gotten loose in the fall. Special earring, too. A small golden angel, a diamond in the place of its head. Whatever this was, it wasn't a robbery, for her wallet was still in her purse, and those earrings also cost a pretty penny. Even her wedding ring was still on her finger. And as he stood, his face grim, he announced, "We better have a chat with Mr. Bloom. Tell him the bad news."

It wasn't one of his favorite tasks, but someone had to do it, and since he might give them some indication what his wife was doing here, there might be something gleaned from the interview. "Maybe we can have another shot at Brigham Shatwell," he told Pierre and watched the man's eyes light up.

Yep, the guy had a sweet tooth, all right.

And when finally they were on their way back to Manhattan, he found his mind returning to the previous day and to Ernestine Flummox, for no reason whatsoever suddenly wondering what the woman was doing right now.

Chapter 20

*A*s it so happened, Ernestine was at that exact moment thinking about Sam. She was on her way to the office, after sharing her concern about Gran with her two sisters. They'd decided to hold off on turning the garden into a pool and Jacuzzi area and the greenhouse into a garage, 'with a nice big slab of concrete,' as Gran had added before she ran out the door for some errand.

Breakfast had been an unmitigated disaster, as Edelie had tried to whip up something edible by using her magic skills and had failed spectacularly.

She loved watching the Food Network for inspiration, but she could have fooled Ernestine. What she'd come up with were fritters of some kind that looked and tasted—according to Strel—like deep-fried rats' guts—not that she would know what rats' guts would taste like, of course. Disgusting, was the consensus, not to mention that Ernestine, as a vegetarian, didn't eat rat. Though Estrella, who wasn't a vegetarian, seemed equally repulsed by the savory dish.

When it was all over, tiny bits of rats' guts were covering the floor, walls and ceiling, as if an explosion had taken place in a rats' guts processing plant, if such a thing existed, which Ernestine sincerely hoped it didn't, for even though she wasn't particularly fond of the critters, they were still part of the animal kingdom and as such shouldn't be subjected to critter fritter cruelty.

And as she rode the subway into Manhattan, she found her thoughts suddenly wandering to Sam Barkley again, and wondered what he would have to say about this whole mess with Gran. Would he agree that something really weird was going on? Or would he simply ascribe it to that knock on the head the woman had suffered, like Estrella did? Strel insisted Gran would simply 'snap out of it' sooner or later, and go back to normal, but Ernestine shared Edie's pessimistic view that something else was going on.

Gran's entire personality had changed overnight, and then there was the fact that she couldn't practice magic anymore, which was even more worrisome. She'd always been the one to protect the three sisters and the house from being overrun by powerful forces of evil, so where did that leave them now? Vulnerable and weak and prone to attack, which wasn't good.

And now she wanted to tear down her own life's work and destroy the flower garden and greenhouse that were as close to her heart as the triplets.

Ernestine had been thinking hard about what spells it would take to turn the garden into a pool and the greenhouse into a garage and frankly she didn't have a clue. She wasn't a very talented witch at all, and neither were her two sisters, so why would Gran want them of all people to fix the garden?

And as she sat gazing at the man seated across from her, she thought he looked remarkably like Sam. Then she decided not to dwell on the detective. For one thing, she'd never see him again, not unless someone was suddenly murdered at Safflower

House—which she sincerely hoped would never happen—and secondly, he obviously was a Neanderthal who hated her.

She got off at her usual stop and joined the throng of commuters to reach the office building where Boodle, Jag, Lack & Noodle had made their home.

Arriving on the tenth floor, where Spear Boodle, son of founder and partner Nixon Boodle, held court, she popped her head into Mr. Boodle's corner office to say hi and was surprised to find him absent from the scene.

Moving over to Spear's personal secretary Mary Winters, she asked, "Isn't Spear in today?"

The woman looked at her owlishly through horn-rimmed glasses not unlike her own and lowered her voice to a conspiratorial whisper. "Oh, he's in, all right. He's in the conference room with the police!"

"The police? What do they want?"

"Apparently something's going on with one of his clients," Mary said, her voice still down to a whisper. She wasn't merely a remarkably able secretary but also a remarkable force of gossip around the office.

"Which client?" she asked, a sense of foreboding stealing over her.

Mary looked around as if expecting Boodle, Jag, Lack & Noodle to suddenly jump up from behind the office ficus and drag her gossiping ass away.

"Lyndon Bloom." Then she frowned. "Wasn't he the one you had that interview with yesterday?"

Her heart now beating a mile a minute, she asked, "Did something happen to Mr. Bloom?"

"Not to Mr. Bloom," she said. "But to Mrs. Bloom."

"What..." She gulped a little. "What happened?"

"Didn't you hear the news? She was murdered! They found her body just now. Strangled on some deserted construction site." Her eyes went wide, an effect magnified by her glasses. "They say it was the invisible choker!"

As Ernestine hurried into her own office, she tried to calm her frayed nerves. She plunked down in her chair, placed her purse on the desk, and stared before her, unable to move. She'd talked to Mr. Bloom yesterday, and he'd been telling her all those stories about how his wife had cheated on him. What were the odds that she was murdered today? Could he have done it himself? But why would he go and do a horrible thing like that?

She almost yelled out when the door to her office suddenly opened, and Spear Boodle stuck his head in. "Police want a word with you, Ernestine. Do you have a moment? In the conference room," he added when Ernestine quickly got up and hurried over. He grabbed the legal pad and pen from her hands. "You won't need those," he said grimly, and then jerked his head in the direction of the conference room, indicating she better hurry on up.

And as she moved as fast as her heels allowed, the parquet floor noisily clacking under her feet, she felt a distinct flush rising up from her chest, along her neck, and coloring her cheeks. Oh, God, she thought. Was she going to have to tell the police all about the weird faces she'd pulled yesterday? Had Lyndon Bloom complained about her? What was she going to say? She couldn't tell them about the cheating with twenty-four lovers, could she? Didn't that fall under the client-lawyer confidentiality thingy?

She arrived at the conference room, coincidentally the same one where she'd terrified Mr. Bloom, and knocked before a gruff voice told her, "Come!"

She strode in and saw a broad-shouldered man gazing out the window, his back to her. There was a second person present, a smallish man who was eating a donut and looked a little bored. She seemed to recognize him.

"I'm, um, I'm Ernestine Flummox," she announced, "You wanted me?"

The man turned around, and she gasped when she saw that it was... Sam Barkley! He gave her a look of surprise. "I'll be damned. Miss Flummox."

She nodded, her frayed nerves becoming even more frayed. "Detective."

He gestured at a chair. "Close the door and take a seat, please."

"Take a donut," the little man suggested, indicating a box of donuts.

"No, thanks. I'm fine," she said, trying to keep the tremor from her voice.

"So," Detective Barkley began, "what's all this I hear about you and Lyndon Bloom? Your boss told me you interviewed the guy yesterday?"

She raised her chin. "I'm afraid I can't discuss any part of that conversation, Detective Barkley. The lawyer-client privilege prevents me."

"Cut the crap, Miss Flummox," he growled. He'd strode over to her side of the table and was now towering over her. "Like I said, I talked to your boss, and he assured me of your full cooperation. In case you didn't know, Mrs. Bloom's body was found an hour ago. Murdered. We're still trying to track down her husband, and anything you can tell us is highly appreciated."

She slumped a bit, the fight leaving her again. "Of course."

The detective took a seat on the edge of the table and folded his arms, bearing down on her with the full force of his personality. It made her feel distinctly out of sorts. "So you're handling the Bloom divorce?"

"Yes, we are. That is to say, Mr. Boodle is. I was interviewing Mr. Bloom to gather some preliminary information. I'm one of his legal secretaries, you see."

"So what did the guy have to say?" And before she could respond, he held up his hand. "And don't give me that lawyer... client privilege crap again."

She bit her lip. "Yes, Detective. Of course."

"A woman's been murdered," he growled and tapped the table smartly.

"Did he—did he kill her?"

"Too soon to tell," he allowed, then placed a small recording device in front of her, and pressed record. "Talk to me, Miss Flummox. Take me through the interview and leave out nothing. Your loyalty right now is to truth and justice, not to your client. Do I make myself clear?"

"Yes, of course," she said, eyeing the device and wondering if this was how it felt to be in a courtroom, questioned on the stand. Even though she'd wanted to be a lawyer her whole life, she'd never been in this situation before, and it wasn't a very pleasant experience. And as she took Detective Barkley through the interview, she did decide to leave out the part about pulling strange faces at Mr. Bloom in an effort to appear more appealing. She didn't feel this would further the cause of 'truth and justice' to any distinct degree.

"So he said his wife cheated on him no less than twenty-four times, huh? And she told him every time? Even made him shake hands with her lovers?"

"That's what he said."

Sam whistled through his teeth. "Twenty-four motives for murder."

"He also said he now regretted staying married to her for so long, but at the time he didn't feel he could leave her."

"So the guy shook hands with his wife's lovers and still didn't think to divorce her?" He tapped his teeth with his pen. "Did you ask him why?"

"I think mainly because he was afraid to be alone," she intimated.

He fixed her with a curious look. "I'm not a shrink, but that sounds like aberrant behavior. If someone did that to me, I'd divorce her so fast her head would spin."

She smiled. "Those were my thoughts exactly."

"Are you in a relationship right now, Miss Flummox?"

Her lips pursed. "As a matter of fact I'm not." She gave him a hard stare. "Does this have any bearing on your investigation, Detective Barkley?"

The little guy smirked at this, even as he sank his teeth into a donut, and Barkley blinked. "No, it doesn't," he admitted stiffly. Then he finally stood. "Thank you for your cooperation, Miss Flummox. If something else comes to mind, give me a call, all right?" He handed her a card, and she tucked it away.

"This interview is over?"

"Yeah, I guess it is. Unless there's more you want to tell me?"

"No," she said, greatly relieved. "No, that was the extent of the conversation I had with Mr. Bloom yesterday."

"I'll leave you to it, then," he said, extending a hand.

She shook it, and was surprised how warm and large it was, and how strong. And as she gazed into his eyes, she saw a twinkle of humor there that surprised her even more. She'd figured the man was a knucklehead, gruff and rude and unpleasant, but he was more intelligent than she'd taken him for.

"Thank you, Miss Flummox."

"Ernestine, please."

"Just call me Sam. How's your grandmother, by the way?"

"She's... fine," she lied, not wanting to involve Sam in the Gran mess.

"That's great to hear. Frankly, I was a little worried when I saw Ronny Mullarkey with your grandmother. Seriously, that guy's bad news." He shook his head. "If I were you, I'd keep your granny far away from him."

"I will, detective—Sam. Thank you for the advice."

"You're welcome... Ernestine."

And after a quick smile and a nod to the other detective, who was still munching donuts, she left the room. Her head was spinning a little, and this time it wasn't from nervousness but from something else entirely...

Chapter 21

*E*delie was in a funk. For the second day in a row she'd arrived late to work, and this time, Ginger had told her, there would be no more reprieves. One more incident and she was out. Apparently, it had been quite the busy morning, and customers had been lining up on the sidewalk. When finally she'd managed to make the kitchen look presentable again that morning, she'd known she'd never make it to work on time, so she'd called Ginger and told her Gran was sick, and she needed to take her to the hospital.

It was a feeble excuse, and Ginger hadn't accepted it.

The worst part was that now she'd finally proven to herself and her family that she couldn't cook. She loved cooking, like Estrella loved singing and Ernestine loved the law, but she simply sucked at it. They all sucked at what they loved, and even more at being witches. They were simply three losers.

Maybe it was time to drop the dream of being a chef, she thought as she handed a businessman with perfectly coiffed hair his preferred caffeine treat. Maybe she should just accept that she would be a coffee shop girl for the rest of her life, never fulfilling her dream of being the next cooking sensation.

Then her thoughts returned to Gran. What was the matter with her?! The woman was completely out of control, as if that bump on the head had somehow rendered her mentally unbalanced and had turned her into a completely different person. Now she didn't even like flowers anymore!

She looked up when a handsome guy tried to attract her attention.

"Two coffees to go and what do you have by way of pastry?" he asked. "My partner has a sweet tooth," he added, giving her a comical grin.

Partner? He didn't look gay, but then you never knew, of course. But then she caught a flash of his badge. Duh. He was a cop, of course.

"What brings you out here, officer?" she asked as she prepared him two large coffees and picked up the tongs to start fishing around for pastry.

"Oh, you know, the usual," he said, leisurely leaning his large frame against the counter. "Mayhem and murder."

"Mayhem and murder in Manhattan, huh? Now that's a first."

He grinned. "Yeah, well, it's all these banker types lurking around and stalking the streets. Murdering maniacs, every last one of 'em."

"Should I be afraid now? I mean, this is their hunting ground."

He gave her a mock serious look. "As long as they're properly caffeinated they're not so dangerous. It's when they don't get their daily dose of coffee that you have to watch out. They can get really vicious when that happens."

"Is that your professional opinion, officer?"

He gave her a grin and a wink. "Public service announcement from your friendly neighborhood cop, honey."

"I'll keep it in mind," she said, as she offered him a baggie with two chocolate cupcakes. "Here, let me know if your partner likes them."

"Will do," he said, tipping an imaginary cap as he took the paper baggie and the cup holder.

She watched him stride out and heaved a wistful sigh. If only she could bag that kind of man...

"Hey! Edelie!"

"Yes, Ginger," she said automatically.

"Stop ogling the customers. Serve them instead!" her boss yelled as she pointed to two more people waiting in the queue.

"Yes, Ginger," she repeated, trying to control her eyes' habit to roll around every time Ginger opened her mouth.

With the coffeehouse being this busy and Ginger in a lousy mood, there was no way she'd be allowed to try out any new experiments. Not that she felt like doing so. After everything that had happened, food experiments were the furthest thing from her mind right now.

* * *

Sam strode from Brigham Shatwell's, coffees and cupcakes in hand, when he suddenly remembered something. He quickly returned to the coffeehouse, trying to draw the attention of the coffee girl. "Um, Miss!" he bellowed.

The woman turned, eyeing him with large eyes that seemed shadowed somehow. "Edelie," she said, and only now did he check her name tag.

He frowned. "Are you by any chance related to Ernestine Flummox?"

"She's my sister," the woman said. "Why? Is there a problem, officer?"

"No, not a problem," he said with a grin. "Just an awfully big coincidence. I was just talking to your sister twenty minutes ago."

"About Gran?" Edelie asked, eyes wide. "Something happened to her?"

"No, no, not about your grandmother. A different matter entirely. I was at your house yesterday, though. Your sister might have told you about that?"

"Yes—yes, she told me. Though I didn't know it was you."

"Yeah, every time someone's granny goes missing, I'm the one they call."

He got her to smile at that, and he was glad. She looked better when she smiled. "Look," he said, "I forgot to ask for some cream. My partner..."

"He doesn't like his coffee black," she supplied. "Got it." She quickly added some cream to his bag, and he gave her a nod in appreciation.

"Say hi to your sister for me," he said, "and tell her that if you guys need anything, anything at all, just give me a call."

"Will do, officer."

"Detective," he said. "Detective Barkley. But you can call me Sam."

"Edelie," she said. "Though my sisters call me Edie."

"Have a great one, Edie!" he said, striding out.

She was a great gal, he thought as he left the coffeehouse for the third time that morning. Completely different from her sisters but very nice. Then he berated himself. What was up with him? Why did he keep hitting on those Flummox sisters? Good thing he hadn't been flirting with Estrella, or else it would have been three for three. And shaking his head, he stepped into the car and handed Pierre his coffee and cupcakes. That would keep him happy.

"Where to now?" Pierre asked, licking his lips as he checked out the cupcakes.

"Let's take another stab at Lyndon Bloom, shall we?"

"The guy finally turn up?"

"He turned up all right. Spent the night in Paris, apparently."

"Paris! Good for him."

"Yeah," he said as he started up the trusty Crown Vic. "Living the good life, buddy. Living the good life."

"Not so good if his wife got murdered," Pierre put in.

His fingers paused on the ignition. "Yeah, you're probably right. Having your wife killed, even though she's almost your ex, probably isn't much fun."

Not that he would know. He'd never been married, so no wives or ex-wives to worry about. Then he put the car in gear and, for the second time that morning, peeled away from the curb, leaving a hubcap in his wake.

Chapter 22

*E*strella was sitting cross-legged on her bed, phone in hand. Her brow was furrowed and her mood low. She'd called half a dozen production companies but none of them had any work for her. Either a sudden crisis had broken out in the advertising business—and overnight at that—or they'd all been informed about her latest stunt and preferred to keep their studios intact and not demolished by her surprisingly muscular vocal shenanigans.

She brought her phone to her ear again, a little bit worried about the bill she was racking up. The moment the call connected, she affected her most chipper voice.

"Boon? Estrella. I wanted you to be the first to know I have an opening in my schedule, so if you wanted to book me now, I'm pretty sure I could squeeze you in."

"Estrella, yeah, hi," a laid-back voice sounded. Then a long pause, followed by, "Look, I'm sorry to be the bearer of bad news, babe, but I got a call from Mike last night. Something about you demolishing his studio?"

"That was an accident," she was quick to say. "And I promise you it will never happen again, Boon."

"Yeah, well, I'm sure you didn't mean no harm, babe, but the thing is, this is a very small industry, and word kinda spreads fast, you know..."

She closed her eyes and cursed inwardly. "Don't tell me I'm being blacklisted, Boon."

"Yeah. Yeah, basically you are. I'm sorry, Strel. I always loved working with you. You may not have the greatest voice, but you're way cool. Sorry."

After the call disconnected, she sat staring at the wall for a bit, then dropped the phone and flopped back on the bed, her arms under her head.

So she was being blacklisted, huh? How about that? She stared at the ceiling, taking in the sparkly lights she'd hung up there ten Christmases ago and had left up ever since. She loved Christmas. It was her favorite time of the year. Always had been, always would. If she could have Christmas year round, she'd be the happiest almost-twenty-one-year-old in the world.

So she wasn't going to be a singer and she wasn't going to be a voice-over artist. What was left? She could be a stylist, of course, like Kim. If only she could manage to keep her own clothes in her own wardrobe and not go flouncing around the house, harassing her sisters and disturbing their sleep.

And then she heard the door slam downstairs and sat up. Gran was back! It had to be her, for Ernestine and Edelie were still at work—unless they'd both been blacklisted as well, which she didn't think was likely.

"Gran!" she yelled as she hopped from the bed. "Wanna hear the latest?"

But when she arrived on the landing and peered over the old wooden balustrade she saw no one. She decided to go check and hopped down the stairs, her brand-new yellow Crocs silent on the red runner. When she arrived in the hallway, she saw no sign of Gran. She wasn't in the living room, the parlor or the kitchen either, and when she checked the terrace, she didn't see her in the garden. So she returned to the kitchen, filling a glass of water at the tap and taking a big gulp. All this talking to producers had made her seriously thirsty. And when she was tipping back the glass of water, she noticed a spot on the ceiling and groaned. Probably a bit of Edie's rat bits.

So she dragged a chair from the breakfast nook to the sink and stood on top of it, trying to reach the spot. She was the shortest of the three sisters, and she couldn't quite reach the ceiling. So she stood on her tippy-toes and slapped a kitchen towel at the recalcitrant piece of frittered rats' guts. It finally peeled away from the ceiling and dropped on her face.

"Yuck!" she yelled and frantically brushed it off in a flurry of movement.

And that's when she noticed that the ceiling was vibrating and she stood stock-still, listening intently. It was a soft rhythmic tapping. And since Gran's room was located just over the kitchen, it was obvious what the source of the tapping was. But how had Gran managed to sneak past her?

She hopped off the chair and trotted into the hallway, then up the stairs, humming a little tune, characteristically off-key. She arrived upstairs and strode over to the door to Gran's room, and listened for a moment. Someone was moving around in there, all right, but why would Gran sneak into her room like this, when she knew Estrella was home? Usually, she dropped by for a chat or called out to join her in the kitchen for a cup of tea and biscuits.

And that's when she heard it.

A hoarse chuckle, in a voice that was definitely not Gran's!

Someone was in there with her! Someone whose voice she'd

never heard before. And for some strange reason a sudden fear gripped her, and her hand, which had been poised to knock, lowered and dropped down to her side, and she took a step away from the door. Something very weird was going on. Ernestine and Edelie were right. Something was wrong with Gran.

But before she could return to her own room, the door to Gran's room was suddenly yanked open, and the woman appeared, glancing around suspiciously. When she caught sight of her granddaughter, a smile crept up her face, but it was a smile of such fakeness Estrella had to suppress a groan.

"Hello there, dear," said Gran in the sweetest possible tone. "Were you looking for me?"

"I was," she admitted, then took a step closer, trying to look past Gran into her room. "Do you have a visitor in there?"

Gran blocked her view, and said, "No, of course not. Just me, myself and I. How was breakfast? Did Edie fix you guys up something nice and tasty?"

"Edelie fixed us up the worst breakfast in the history of the world," she said, her stomach turning at the recollection.

"Oh, that's such a pity," said Gran vaguely. "But she did whip up something, didn't she? I can feel it." She held out a hand as if trying to determine if it was windy or not. "Yes, I can definitely feel the magic in the air."

"Yeah, I guess she did her best."

"That's just wonderful," said Gran, rubbing her hands with glee. "Now we're just waiting for Ernestine to perform her magic, and we're all set."

"All set for what?" she asked, puzzled.

"Oh, that's nothing for you to worry about, dear," said Gran, patting her hideous hair absentmindedly. "Now run along. Granny has some stuff to take care of." And promptly she returned to her room and slammed the door shut. This time, Estrella heard the key turning in the lock, and she gasped. Gran never locked her door! What the heck was going on?!

Then an idea occurred to her. She remembered Edelie once telling her there were secret passageways that ran all through the house. She'd been using them for years and liked to curl up in the walls to read one of those depressing novels she loved so much. Estrella had never taken an interest, either in the novels or the passageways, being more the outdoorsy type, and neither had Ernestine, who didn't do creepy and bug-infested. But maybe now was a good time to find out if there was a way to peek into Gran's room.

Returning to her own room, she picked her phone from the bed, and while she waited for the call to connect, strode to the window and looked out across the street. All the houses on Nightingale Street were old and well-maintained, with big gardens and lots of space, which was exceptional in this part of the city, but none of them were as nice as Safflower House. At least as long as Gran didn't insist on turning the garden into a patio and the greenhouse into a garage for this new 'muscle car' obsession of hers...

Edelie finally picked up with a morose, "Yo."

"Edie!" she hissed, "Gran is behaving weird again. This time she's locked herself up in her room. And I could swear there's a guy in there with her!"

"Yeah, what else is new?" Edie asked, and Estrella could hear the hustle and bustle of the coffeehouse and someone yelling, "Edelie! Customers!"

Poor Edelie, Estrella thought. She wasn't having a lot of fun at work.

"I can't talk now," her sister said. "My psycho boss is acting up again."

"I need you to tell me how to get into those secret passageways you like so much. I want to find out what Gran is up to!" she quickly told her sister.

"Later," Edelie said gruffly, then promptly disconnected.

"Aargh!" Estrella cried in frustration and dropped down on the bed. If things didn't go back to normal very quickly now, she was going to murder someone! Which suddenly reminded her of Detective Barkley. Maybe she should give him a call? Something weird was going on with Gran, and it had all started when she met this Ronny Mullarkey guy. Maybe he was the one in there with Gran! Maybe he'd put a spell on her!

Detective Barkley... She pictured the handsome cop and felt her stomach go weak all of a sudden. He was gruff and rude but also intensely and irresistibly virile. She was sure that if she called him right now and told him Ronny was in the house, doing weird and suspicious stuff with Gran he'd come right over! Or would he? He hadn't seemed particularly keen the previous day, expecting dead bodies where no dead bodies were.

No, the fact that Gran had taken up entertaining untrustworthy men in her room hardly seemed like a good enough reason to call the police...

"Aargh!" she groaned again and jumped up from the bed. Suddenly she wanted to get out of there, and started changing into her running clothes. She needed some fresh air—and to put this entire situation out of her mind. Edelie and Ernestine would be back in a couple of hours, and they could decide what to do then. Right now she needed to work off some of her frustration!

So she called out, "Going for a run, Gran!" and raced down the stairs, then out of the house. Safflower House had always been her home, and she loved the place, but the moment she closed the door behind her, such a wave of relief washed over her that she was momentarily floored. What was going on?

Chapter 23

"I just had to get away," Lyndon said, wringing his hands incessantly.

The guy seemed a nervous wreck, Sam thought, his face white as chalk and his eyes red and bleary. He was one of the city's best-known financiers, and one of the mayor's friends—he'd funded his last campaign—and there were even rumors circulating he might run for mayor himself when his friend's term was up. This divorce had taken a huge toll on him, however.

"So you're telling me you spent the night in Paris?"

"I have an apartment in the 7th arrondissement, near the Eiffel Tower."

"Of course you have."

"You can check my plane's arrival time with the airport. I keep all my planes at the private airstrip, but flight data is all logged in by the pilot."

"Of course," he repeated, wondering how many people he knew who had private planes—plural. It was a very short list: Lyndon Bloom. Well, that put him in the clear for his wife's murder, of course. Not that he'd ever seriously considered the possibility he was involved. The case had all the hallmarks of the invisible choker, and this guy didn't look like a serial killer.

"Did you and your wife break up a long time go?"

"Only last month," he said, nervously bringing a hand to his face. "But we'd been living apart for almost a year. She had her own place, and we rarely spoke."

"So the divorce didn't come as a surprise?"

"No, not really. I'd been giving it a lot of thought, and finally decided that I was better off without her. Living apart had shown me I could live without her, so..." He broke off and rubbed his face with his hands. "I can't believe she's gone!" Then he looked up, eyes pleading. "Who did this to her, Detective?"

"We're working on the supposition the invisible choker is involved."

Lyndon's eyes went wide. "The invisible choker! Not that... monster!"

"I'm afraid so. Unfortunately the murder of your wife fits the same MO."

"But why? What's the connection?"

"Well," Sam said, settling back, "Your wife fits the profile to a T, I'm afraid. All the victims so far were between twenty-five and thirty-five, all beautiful, highly successful and prominent figures of society." There was another feature they shared, but he didn't know if it was a good idea to get into that right now.

They were conducting the interview in Lyndon Bloom's apartment, overlooking Central Park. It was probably the nicest pad he'd ever set foot in. From the furniture to the furnishings, everything looked like it had cost a small fortune, which it probably did. Parts of Lyndon's art collection were on display here that any collector would salivate over, and he figured Lyndon must have a state-of-the-art security system to keep the bad guys out.

He had to hand it to the guy, though, the place was also cozy. You could feel that actual people lived here and that they'd made this place their home. He wondered how much of it was Selena and how much Lyndon.

"There is one other trait they all shared," he finally said after a quick look at Pierre. "All of the victims reportedly dabbled in the occult."

"The occult?"

"That's right. Your wife took an active interest in the paranormal."

"But that was just a hobby. I mean, Selena loved to consult tarot cards and palmists and was into Kabbalah, but that's hardly dabbling in the occult."

"According to our information, she did a lot more than that. She and a group of her friends used to meet in Central Park from time to time to..." He eyed Pierre again, but the man was studying a sculpture of a swan with particular interest. "... to dance naked under the light of the full moon."

Lyndon laughed, an astonished look on his face. "You've got to be kidding me!"

"No, we have it from a reliable source. Selena and her friends reportedly did this because they believed it would help them stay young forever."

"Now that I can believe," Lyndon said, nodding. "She was obsessed with staying young. She hated growing older and battled every wrinkle with a ferocity perhaps better reserved for a worthier cause. I didn't think her devotion to youth and beauty went that far, however. Who told you this?"

He checked his notebook. They'd interviewed two of Selena's friends before finally being granted an interview with the great Lyndon Bloom. "A woman called Zada Fundus and another one called Ola O'Regano."

"Yes, they were two of Selena's best friends."

"They both took part in these rituals, along with four other women."

"Dancing naked under the full moon," said Lyndon, that look of astonishment still on his face. "I never would have thought Selena was into that kind of stuff."

"Well, that's the link that connects her to the other victims. All of them were into the occult to some extent, whether it was trying to get in touch with their ancestors through a medium or toying with witchcraft, they all believed in the paranormal—in a higher power not of this world. Hell, I don't know," he said, raking his hand through his hair. "I don't even know if it's important. Just one of those things we hope will help us catch this murdering maniac."

"I hope you catch him," said Lyndon sincerely. "I loved my wife, in spite of everything. It was one of the reasons I found it so hard to file for divorce."

"Yes, we spoke to Ernestine Flummox from your lawyer's firm."

At the mention of the name, a look of fear flitted over Lyndon's face.

"She told us about the interview you had with her yesterday."

"Yes, Spear Boodle called me this morning about your request. I gave him my permission, of course. I do hope you will keep my interview... private?"

"Of course. Nothing that was discussed goes beyond my colleague or me."

Lyndon eyed Pierre curiously. He seemed to wonder about him.

"Pierre is one of those strong, silent types," Sam felt compelled to point out. "Anyway, I think that concludes our business here this morning. If there's anything else you can think of, just give Pierre or me a call, will you?"

"Of course," said Lyndon, then added hesitantly, "My interview with Ernestine Flummox yesterday... I don't know if this is relevant at all, but she kept making the weirdest faces at me."

"Faces?"

"Yes. First she was grinning like an ape, and when I pointed this out to her, her features morphed into the most hideous and murderous expression I've ever seen on the face of a woman, or any human being for that matter." He shivered even as he told the story. "She frankly gave me the creeps, Detective Barkley, and I've asked Spear not to have any more dealings with the woman." He lowered his voice. "She's evil. Pure, unadulterated evil."

Sam would have laughed hysterically if Lyndon hadn't appeared deadly serious. "Well, I'll add it to my considerations, Mr. Bloom," he said after a pause, fighting to keep a straight face. "Though I very much doubt Miss Ernestine Flummox has anything to do with your wife's murder."

"You have to admit it's very suspicious, Detective. This obviously homicidal woman interviewed me yesterday about Selena, and this morning she's found dead!" He eyed him seriously. "If I were you I'd definitely add her to your list of suspects. I'm telling you; the woman is dangerous!"

As they were riding the elevator down, Sam and Pierre's eyes met, and they both burst out laughing. Highly inappropriate, of course, but it was simply one of those moments when stuff gets so weird that you can't help but have a good laugh. Ernestine Flummox the invisible choker. Yeah, right!

Chapter 24

*E*strella was pumping her arms and legs furiously. She'd reached the local park and was now running full out, letting go of the frustrations of the past twenty-four hours by pushing her body to its limits. She loved to run, and whenever the opportunity presented itself would put on her running gear and put in ten miles, listening to her favorite music, and occasionally belting along with the music. Today, however, she was silent, fearing that part of the spell she'd used on herself the day before might still be in her system, and induce the trees to shed their leaves and the whole world to come crashing down around her, like Mike Hognose's studio window.

And she was just doing her second lap around the park, meeting the same people she usually met, old folk and mothers pushing strollers, when she caught sight of a curious phenomenon. The sky overhead had suddenly darkened to a degree, and it now looked as if it might rain. Which was weird, as it had been sunny all morning, and the forecast said nothing about rain.

Trusting her weather app more than her own eyes, she kept on running, thinking it would blow over, but it didn't. Quite the opposite, in fact: dark clouds gathered overhead, and suddenly the park was empty and she was the only person still doing laps.

Day had suddenly turned into night, and the darkness around her was oppressive, and then the first drops fell and they were fat and cold and within seconds she was soaked to the skin!

She wanted to make a run for it and get home, but a sudden flash of lightning told her it might be a better idea to wait out the storm by hiding under one of the big trees. Being struck by lightning was not what she had in mind! But the wind picked up, and rain was now lashing at her horizontally, the whole world morphing into this terrible storm, pummeling her ferociously. And then she saw the small tunnel under the hill at the heart of the park, and she dashed over. She could hide there until the storm blew out.

There was an urban legend that the tunnel had been dug by trolls or goblins and that they still lived down here. It was one of the reasons most people gave it a wide berth. She'd never given much credence to the story, but now that she was standing in the dark tunnel, watching nature unleash its demons upon the world, she was starting to get a very bad feeling.

And it was then that a gruff voice behind her barked, "You have a hard time listening, don't you, Estrella Flummox?"

She spun around and saw that Tavish Mildew had returned. He was still dressed in black from head to foot, only now his brow was furrowed and his expression as dark as his outfit. Yesterday on the bus he'd been a jolly old camper compared to the way he was regarding her now.

"What do you mean?" she asked. "We tried to talk to Gran but she's in such a weird mood that—"

"Did I tell you to talk to your grandmother?!" he thundered. "No! All I said was to find Joshua and stop him before he stops you. Permanently!"

"But who is this Joshua?" she asked helplessly. "And where can we find him? You have to give me something to go on here,

Tavish. And who are *you*, for that matter? I mean, who's to say you're not the bad guy in this story?"

He didn't even crack a smile. "You're going through a tough time, Estrella, and so are your sisters, and you have to accept there is a reason."

She wiped the rain from her brow. This guy was simply too much. "The reason is that we're the worst three witches in the world! Not just that, but I'm the worst singer, Ernestine the worst lawyer person, and Edelie the worst cook! I think it's safe to say the Flummox sisters are the world's biggest losers!"

"No!" he boomed. "There's one thing you're *very* good at. Your mission."

She laughed miserably. "Our *mission*? Do I look like Frodo the Hobbit to you? I don't have a mission! I don't even have a *job*!"

His face was still a mask of seriousness. "If you don't do as instructed, your lives will be over," he said, "very soon now, and I cannot tolerate that."

"Why?" she challenged, getting sick and tired of this guy. "Why do you care so much? You don't even know us!"

"I took you on as my sacred charges a long time ago," he said, his voice softening, "and I'll be damned if I'm going to forsake this promise now."

"Promise? Sacred charges? Can't you talk English for once?"

"Let me be blunt, then. I promised your parents that I would take you under my wing when the time came." He nodded, seeing her shocked expression. "And the time has come."

"What are you, like our godfather or something?"

"Something like that," he allowed. "When your parents died you were transferred to your grandmother's care, with the understanding that I would keep a close eye on you when you reached the age of consent."

"We reached the age of consent a long time ago, buddy."

"The age when you come into your own and accept your heritage."

"Yeah, I know all about that, but if you hadn't noticed, we're not exactly the most talented witches in the world."

"I'm not talking about being witches. I'm talking about..." A clash of thunder momentarily drowned out his voice, but Estrella could have sworn it sounded a lot like... thieves.

"Did you just say thieves?"

A strange look had stolen over his face. "Your father was a great thief, and your mother a powerful witch. The moment they joined forces they were... magical. Your father's life might have ended in ruin, but your mother was his saving grace. Together they turned their profession into an art form."

She shook her head, droplets sprinkling in all directions. This wasn't making any sense. "You're telling me our parents were a bunch of thieves?"

"Not merely thieves," he said, a devoted expression softening his features. "Your parents had witchy fingers. They only stole from people who deserved it. People who took what didn't belong to them. And they did it by using your father's burgling skills and your mother's grasp of ancient witchcraft."

"Magical Robin Hoods, huh?" She was suddenly feeling a little faint, and the fact that she was wet and shivering had nothing to do with it. "But why didn't Gran ever tell us about this?"

"Because your grandmother never approved of your father. She accused your mother of turning her back on her family by marrying a common crook. And then when your parents died, it seemed to prove her point..."

"How did they die?" she asked, posing the ultimate question.

"Ask your grandmother. She knows."

"I did. She said they died in an accident. A car crash."

"They died in an accident, all right, but cars didn't feature into it."

"Look, enough with the games. Either you tell me what happened to my parents or..." She stomped her foot, trying to figure out a way to make this guy talk already. This was why she didn't like TV shows. They always made you wait weeks for the big reveal! "Or I'll simply walk!" One eye at the storm told her this was an empty threat, however, but she had to give it a try.

"They died on a job," he finally said after a long pause. "They burgled the lair of a powerful warlock, and they perished because they weren't prepared."

She stared at the man. "But why..."

"They wanted to take something from him that didn't belong to him. Something he'd stolen and was using for his personal satisfaction." He was nodding even as she was forming the words. "Yes, that warlock was Joshua, and he's back to finish the job he started twenty years ago. He killed your parents and now he's coming for you... and your grandmother."

She'd clasped her hands to her face. "Oh. My. God."

"Do you see now how important it is not to get distracted? This is your mission in life, Estrella. Yours and your sisters'. Tread the path your parents took. This is your destiny, even though your grandmother doesn't approve. You're not a singer, nor is Edelie a cook or Ernestine a lawyer. These are merely worldly professions. Your treasures are hidden deep, but once you embrace them, they will bring you fulfillment such as you've never known."

"So we're... thieves?" asked Estrella, flabbergasted.

For the first time, the man smiled. "Not merely thieves. Witchy thieves. Together there's nothing the three of you can't accomplish. And nothing you can't purloin. As long as you don't steal for personal gain, but only to right the wrongs that evil forces have wrought."

"But what about Gran?"

His face darkened again. "Like I told you, this is something you and your sisters have to figure out by yourselves. Your grandmother cannot help you."

"Because Gran is Joshua," she said slowly, remembering his earlier words.

"That's right."

A horrible thought occurred to Estrella. What if Joshua had actually taken possession of Gran and was now holding her hostage?

Another thunderclap tore through the skies, and lightning flashed so powerfully that the world lit up with a blinding light.

"Your birthday is coming up, Estrella. Yours and your sisters'. This is a crucial time for you. You will either perish or persist."

She nodded, understanding dawning. This was all happening because they were coming of age. "So are you a warlock?" she felt compelled to ask.

He nodded slowly. "I am, and it will surprise you to know that once upon a time I was as evil as Joshua. Your mother's compassion and your father's friendship saved me from a horrible fate, and I owe them my eternal gratitude."

She swallowed. "What were they like? Mom and Dad?"

He smiled. "Your mother was the most beautiful, kind and loving woman I've ever had the honor to call my friend, and your father the most honorable and brave man. Together they were unstoppable, until they met Joshua, and perished..." There was more he wanted to say, Estrella could tell, but then his features hardened. "Go now, and tell your sisters. There isn't much time left. Go now and find Joshua and stop him before it's too late." And as he became vaguer and started to disappear like a wisp of fog, she thought he said, "Before your parents' final sacrifice turns out to have been in vain..."

Chapter 25

*E*delie watched her boss from the corner of her eye. The flood of customers had dwindled to a trickle, and frankly she was feeling a little frustrated. She had a genuine crisis on her hands at home and here she was stuck at work. Furthermore, Ginger had been even less amiable than usual, offering only monosyllabic responses whenever Edelie tried to start a conversation. Arriving late two mornings in a row had apparently soured whatever relationship they had.

And it wasn't that Ginger was much of a boss anyway. She was the manager of this particular store, but that didn't make her president of the world now did it? Judging from her behavior, though, she certainly seemed to think so.

After ringing up her final customer, she went back to wiping the counter and cleaning up and was soon lost in thought again. Ever since this black-dressed man had come into her life, things had taken a turn for the worse, she felt, and she wondered if the man was perhaps a warlock, trying to hurt them. Insert himself into their lives and wreak havoc any way he could.

Wasn't that what warlocks did? She didn't know too much about the breed, Gran always reluctant to supply the sisters with information. In fact Gran had always downplayed their witchiness, teaching them only a few simple spells and refusing to take their witchy education to the next level.

Almost as if she was afraid for them to fully come into their own.

She did know that their upcoming twenty-first birthday was something of a milestone. Gran had once let it slip that a witch gets her true powers once she passes that important marker. So would they suddenly turn into capable witches and not the bumbling ones they'd always been? Somehow she doubted it.

"Edelie? A word?" Ginger suddenly asked.

She followed her boss into the small kitchen behind the counter. She was surprised to find that the man she'd served half an hour before was also there.

"Hi," she said, wondering if he was perhaps from corporate, here to do a snap check. They did that sometimes. Mystery shoppers, they called them, and they were sent in to check if service was up to their usual high standards.

"This is James," Ginger began, "and he's going to take over for you."

She raised her eyebrows. "Take over? You mean for today?"

That was nice of Ginger, she thought. She'd told her she had a sick grandmother at home, and now she was going to let her take off earlier.

Ginger pressed her lips together. "No, he's going to take over for you forever." She stressed the last word, drawing out the syllables.

She frowned, still not completely comprehending. "Forever? I don't—"

Ginger groaned and rolled her eyes, then she snapped, "What's so difficult to understand, you pea-brain? You're fired! I'm firing you, that's what this is."

"Fired? But..."

Ginger planted her hand on her hip and launched into a harangue. "You keep showing up late for work, serving customers to you is like having your teeth pulled, judging from that sad look on face, people keep complaining that you serve them lukewarm coffee in half-filled cups, or that you mess up their orders, and what's worse, you shortchange them all the time!" It seemed as if she'd been waiting to give this little speech for ages, and cherished the moment. "Didn't they teach you fricking math in school, Edelie? Huh?"

She blinked. "I don't shortchange," she said weakly. Though maybe she did. Math wasn't her strong suit, and Brigham Shatwell kept changing the prices all the time. "And I definitely don't underserve. That's a lie."

"It's not a lie if several customers complain about it," Ginger pointed out.

She stared at her manager. Was she actually firing her?

"But whatever," said Ginger. "You're out and James is in."

"Sorry about that," the guy murmured, which was actually nice of him.

"I'll have your apron and cap now," Ginger said, holding out her hand.

So Edelie took off her apron and cap and handed them to her boss. Even though she hated this job, she didn't feel any relief. What she felt was humiliation at being treated like this. Basically being fired for not being happy and peppy enough with the customers. Well, she wasn't a happy, peppy person, was she? That didn't make her a bad barista. Did it?

"For the record," James whispered when Ginger momentarily disappeared behind the partition to see if any customers had arrived, "I thought you did great, and you never shortchanged or underserved me."

"Watch out for Ginger," she whispered back. "She's not a nice person."

"I heard that," snapped Ginger, who'd returned at that moment. "And for your information, I *am* a nice person. I'm miss congeniality."

Edelie shrugged. She wasn't about to get into a fight with Ginger.

"Who gave you the opportunity to try out some of your own recipes?"

She shrugged again.

"And who encouraged you to become a pastry chef?"

Edelie was eyeing the door eagerly. She didn't feel like listening to a lecture from someone who'd just fired her for not having the right face.

Suddenly Ginger took her by the shoulders. "You're just not cut out for the service industry, Edelie. Maybe you should try something where you can stay behind the scenes? Where people don't have to look at your sad face all day?" She nodded when Edelie frowned. "You have a very sad face."

"I do not," she protested, though a little bit too feebly.

"Yes, you do. You make me feel sad just watching you."

She stared at James, who was mouthing, 'You don't have a sad face.'

She flashed a brief grin at the guy. Maybe he should be manager here and then she could come back and work for him. She'd like that. He seemed nice.

"Trust me," Ginger continued, "this hurts me more than it hurts you."

"I kinda doubt it," she muttered.

Finally Ginger released her, the lecture over. So she picked up her backpack, and looked around the small coffee shop one last time, then strode out. She'd worked here for over a year, and the place had grown on her. Apart from Ginger being Ginger, she'd had some good times here, especially when she'd been able to experiment in the kitchen and briefly feel like Jamie Oliver. And as she closed the door, she saw that Ginger was giving her a pinkie wave, then gestured to her own face, pulled down into a sad face. Yeah, yeah, she thought. Rub my nose in it, will you? So she stepped out and remembered that saying about one door closing and another door opening.

If only she knew which door that might be she might feel a little less sad.

Chapter 26

*E*rnestine was crunching the numbers again, her face screwed up in concentration. Part of her job as a legal secretary was making sure that the billable hours added up, and she was just going over Spear's most recent numbers when the man himself strode into her office, looking a little grim.

She smiled up at him. As the son of the firm's founder and partner, a big weight had descended upon Spear's shoulders when he'd agreed to follow in his father's footsteps, and she'd always felt he did a great job. Unlike his old man, who was a curmudgeon, Spear was a nice person and a great boss.

He now took a seat in front of her and stared at her for a long time without speaking. She grew a little nervous under his intent stare.

He was a handsome man with movie star good looks, at thirty-two a very eligible bachelor. For a lawyer, he wore his curly brown hair just a little bit too long, and his lips were just a little bit too full to look like a legal shark.

"What's wrong?" she finally asked, giving him her full attention.

"You," Spear said shortly.

"Me? What do you mean?"

"There's been a complaint."

"A complaint?" Her mind instantly shot back to yesterday, when she'd had that awkward scene with Mr. Bloom.

"I talked to Lyndon Bloom this morning. Had to get his permission to share details from the interview you had with him with the cops. He was kind enough to grant us permission, but he also told me something very worrying."

She gulped a little, remembering how Lyndon had practically run out.

"He told me you behaved very strangely yesterday."

Even if she'd wanted to speak, she couldn't, as she sat frozen in her seat.

"I saw you myself, Ernestine, and I noticed the same look that Lyndon was complaining about. He called it, quote, homicidal and maniacal, unquote."

She swallowed. "I—I was just trying to make a good impression."

"I didn't see maniacal and homicidal, Ernestine," Spear said. "All I saw was you trying very hard to offer excellent service to an important client and a client who obviously didn't appreciate that service." He adjusted his jacket. "When I listened to the interview just now, my suspicions were confirmed."

"You listened to the interview?"

She'd forgotten all interviews were recorded for legal reasons, so neither party could accuse the other party of saying things that had never been said.

"Yes, I did, and do you know what I heard?"

She shook her head, staring at her boss and expecting the worst.

"I heard an employee asking all the right questions, and doing exactly what she was supposed to do, making Boodle, Jag, Lack & Noodle proud."

"Thank you, Spear," she said hesitantly. The specter of dismissal was still hovering over her, she knew, but it now seemed unlikely the ax would fall.

Spear sighed. "However, since the client is always right, what I think doesn't matter one iota. I'm afraid we're going to have to let you go, Ernestine." He put his hand on his heart. "Which pains me greatly, I might add."

Her face fell, and so did her mood. "Oh," was all she managed to say.

"Lyndon Bloom is a very important guy in this town and a very important client to this firm, and we can't afford to antagonize him, and at this moment he seems hell-bent on seeing you dismissed from this firm so dismiss you we must." He folded his hands. "But I want to tell you not to be discouraged, Ernestine. I know you as a very conscientious employee, and I'm sure that other opportunities will open up for you in the near future."

"Thank you, Spear," she said in a low voice.

"And contrary to Lyndon's wishes, I'm going to give you a glowing letter of recommendation."

And as he stood, she, too, rose to her feet. Her face suddenly felt hot and cold at the same time, and her heart was beating way too fast. Being fired felt an awful lot like being kicked in the gut, the most horrible thing about the experience the sheer humiliation and feeling she'd failed as a human being.

In spite of Spear's words she suddenly felt smaller than a microbe and worth about as much as an amoeba. She looked up when Spear took her hand and shook it warmly. "I'm sorry, Ernestine," he said, and she could tell his apology was heartfelt. "I'm truly sorry."

Then he was gone, and so was she. Her first job, and perhaps her last. Because in spite of Spear's words she knew it would be hard to come back from this. What law firm would hire her after being fired from this one?

Chapter 27

They met on the subway, which was quite a coincidence. Edelie saw her sister slouching past and was surprised to find Ernestine looking about as downcast as she was feeling. Of course, for her this demeanor was normal, but for proud Ernestine it was quite a departure from her usual look of self-confidence which sometimes bordered on the arrogant.

"Hey, Stien!" she called out when her sister walked past.

Ernestine slowly looked up, and when she saw her sister's sad face, her own sad face became even sadder.

"What happened?" she asked.

"I just got fired. You?"

Ernestine nodded. "Same here."

They stood side by side, two shell-shocked people amongst a seething mass of New Yorkers waiting for the next subway train, staring before them like two zombies waiting for the next brain on legs to heave into view.

"Strel called," Edelie said, suddenly remembering her sister's phone call.

"Oh?" Ernestine asked mutedly and without the faintest interest.

"She said Gran is now locking her door and entertaining male visitors."

"Oh."

"Yeah."

They both seemed to share the view that the world had come to an end and that this little bit of bad news was simply par for the course.

"Spear said he was sorry."

"Ginger wasn't. She said I have a sad face."

"Said if it were up to him I'd still have a job."

"She said just looking at my face made her sad, too."

"Of course it doesn't make a hoot of difference."

"It's my face. I can't change it."

Ernestine looked up. "I like your face."

"Thanks. I like yours."

"Lyndon Bloom didn't. He said I'm maniacal and homicidal."

"I don't think you're homicidal, Stien. I would have noticed if you were."

Ernestine sighed and voiced the question that had been going through Edelie's own mind since her dismissal. "What are we going to do now?"

"Beats me."

"All three of us are out of a job, and Gran has gone gaga."

"Not to mention she wants to turn the house into a pleasure dome."

But then the train arrived, and they both got on, and for the rest of the journey home, they rode in silence. It was so weird, Edelie thought. She and Ernestine had landed their jobs at the same time and had even started on the same day, and had ridden to work together that day. But their schedules were too different, and they'd never ridden the subway together again, until today, their last day. What were the odds? Slim, she would have guessed.

And as they rode on, her mind drifted back to the guy they

all met yesterday. The guy who was so adamant to warn them about Joshua. It wasn't Joshua he should have warned them about, however, but Ginger Peace and Spear Boodle and Mike Hognose. Thanks to them the three Flummox sisters were out of a job, exactly one week before their twenty-first birthdays. And she had a sad face that made other people sad, apparently.

Except her sisters. They liked her face. She folded her fingers into Ernestine's, who gave her a squeeze back. At least they had each other.

* * *

They arrived home and were greeted by a very frazzled-looking Estrella.

"You guys!" she hissed, eyes darting to the stairs and back. "I have to tell you something! But not here!"

And promptly she pushed them out of the door again.

"What's wrong?" Ernestine asked, still a little dazed. She'd never lost a job before, and the experience had been quite a knock to her self-esteem. In fact she couldn't remember ever feeling quite this low.

"Let's go for a walk," Estrella said, pulling them along.

"I'm not in the mood for games," Edelie grumbled. "I just got fired."

"And so was I," Ernestine added.

"But that's great!" was Estrella's surprising response. "That's so great! Now you're free to be who you really are!"

Ernestine closed her eyes, a pained expression on her face. "None of this new age stuff please, Strel. I'm feeling very vulnerable right now."

"I talked to Tavish again," Estrella said, almost manic. But then that was Strel. Even in her darkest hour, she could see the silver lining. Where she got it from, Ernestine didn't know, for both she and Edelie were very different.

"I don't think I want to hear this," Edelie groaned, starting to turn back.

But Estrella pulled her along. "No, you've *got* to hear this!" she insisted. "This is our *future!*"

"We don't have a future, Strel," Edelie said, sounding even more morose than usual, and for once, Ernestine agreed with her gloomy goose sister.

"We are thieves!" suddenly Estrella burst out. "Witchy thieves!"

Both sisters stared at their sibling. Had Estrella, too, taken a nasty fall and hit her head? It seemed quite likely, for her eyes were shining and her expression was ecstatic. Either that or she was high on something.

"Thieves," Ernestine repeated dubiously.

"Witchy thieves," Edelie said with a sigh.

"You guys, you have to believe me! Tavish told me the whole story! Mom was a witch and Dad was a thief and together they were this great team of witchy thieves. They stole from warlocks and other bad... people," she explained, hands gesticulating wildly. "And they only stole stuff to right wrongs and stuff but then they came up against this Joshua character and he..." she gulped, and her voice dropped. "... and then he killed them."

Now she had their full attention, and both Edelie and Ernestine cried, "He did what?!"

She nodded frantically. "Joshua killed Mom and Dad and Gran never told us because she didn't want us to know and go down the same road. She didn't approve when Mom married Dad because he was a thief—one of the best—and she was afraid we'd follow in their footsteps the moment we turned twenty-one but if we don't we're never going to find fulfillment and Joshua is going to come after us and kill us like he did our parents." She paused for breath, and was immediately bombarded with about a thousand questions, and as they walked on, Estrella recounted the strange conversation she had with this warlock who seemed to consider himself their guardian.

"But how can you be sure he's on the level?" Edelie asked.

"Yeah, how do you know he's not lying?"

"There's only one way to know for sure," Estrella pointed out, "and that's by talking to Gran."

They stared at each other for a moment, before Ernestine cried, "Gran's gone off the deep end! There's no way she'll tell us what we want to know."

"We have to try," Estrella said, then told them about her idea to have a look inside Gran's room through the old passageways. "It's the only way to find out what's going on with her." She bit her lip. "I think Joshua has taken control of her. I think he's... possessed her!"

"What?!" Ernestine cried. "That's not even possible!"

"Gran is a powerful witch. No warlock can possess her," Edelie agreed.

"Aren't you forgetting that this is the same warlock who killed our parents?" Estrella pointed out. "And for some reason he's come back for us."

"But why now? Why wait twenty years?" Ernestine asked.

"Didn't you hear a word I said? We're turning twenty-one next week."

"So?" Ernestine asked. "What's the big deal about some stupid birthday?"

Estrella flapped her arms like a chicken before blurting out,

"It's the day we're becoming real witches, you guys! Lots of witchy energy to collect!"

"I still don't get it," Edelie muttered. "Where has this Joshua been for the past twenty years? And how did he manage to kill our parents if they were such a great force for good? And how did he manage to possess Gran if she's supposed to be such a powerful witch? It just doesn't make sense to me."

"None of this makes sense," said Ernestine, sinking onto a low wall that lined one of the nicer houses on the block. She was on the verge of tears now. Not only had she just been fired from the job that was going to be the start of a great career, but warlocks were chasing them and their parents were thieves and some other warlock seemed to believe they were supposed to be thieves, too! "I can't be a thief! I'm gonna be a lawyer! I'm all for truth and justice. I can't just..." She waved her hands helplessly. "... change sides like that!"

Her sisters both sat down beside her and placed their arms around her. "It's all right, honey," said Estrella. "You're not switching sides. We're good thieves. The kind who steal from the bad people and give back to the good."

"Like Robin Hood," said Edelie, though she seemed equally confused.

"But what about you becoming a star singer?" she asked Estrella. "And you becoming a star cook? And me becoming the next Perry Mason or Ben Matlock? What about our dreams? Our hopes? Our future?"

"Our future is sunk," Edelie remarked in her customary upbeat way.

"I'm the worst singer in the world, Stien," Estrella pointed out, "and you're the worst lawyer and Edie the worst cook. Our careers were never going to go anywhere."

"Our careers are a bust," muttered Edelie.

"*This* is our future, you guys," Estrella continued. "Mom and Dad paved the way for us and all we have to do is follow in their footsteps."

"But how do we even know any of this is real?" Ernestine insisted. "All we have is the word of some suspicious warlock we never even met before."

They shared a look. "Gran," Edelie grunted, and Ernestine concurred. They needed to talk to Gran and figure out what was real and what wasn't.

"Where are those passageways, Edie?" Ernestine asked.

"I showed you guys ages ago, don't you remember?"

Both Estrella and Ernestine shook their heads. The only one who was into dark and gloomy places was Edelie. They wouldn't be seen dead in them.

Edelie sighed. "You get in through the basement, and then crawl up."

Ernestine shivered. The basement gave her the creeps. There seemed to be no other way, though, so she agreed when Estrella said, "Let's do it now, you guys. While Gran is in her room. We need to know what she's up to!"

They shook hands on it and then got up. Some of the gloom Ernestine had felt after her dismissal had faded away, she noticed, and even Edelie looked less depressed than before, though with her it was hard to say.

"Let's find out what's going on!" Estrella said with all the fervor of a basketball coach, and perhaps for the first time Ernestine was actually glad to have a sister who was the closest thing to a cheerleader she'd ever known.

"Yes, let's," she agreed, and when finally the trio set foot for Safflower House, they did so with something akin to a spring in their step. Well, except for Edelie, of course, whose feet were simply not equipped for springing.

Chapter 28

*E*delie didn't like this. She'd always dreamed of being a master chef, and here her sister was trying to convince her that her future happiness lay in being a thief instead? That was just crazy talk! But then she knew Estrella was the nuttiest of them all. A person who bewitched their clothes and allowed them to run amok wasn't the person to take career advice from.

She led her sisters into the basement and showed them the big old furnace and the big oil painting hanging right next to it. She'd dubbed it 'Hope,' and it was all black smudges on black canvas. If you looked closely, you could see the outline of a black figure carrying a black torch. Of hope.

Ernestine and Estrella eyed the painting with a critical eye.

"I don't like it," Ernestine remarked. "Too gloomy."

"It is a little dark," Estrella agreed. "Is it cubism?"

"Are you nuts? A kid made that. Or a crazy person. I'm sure if you got a shrink in here he could tell you exactly what was wrong with the artist."

"It's mine," grumbled Edelie, after listening to her sisters with rising indignation. "I decided to put up one of my paintings to hide the hole."

Her two sisters stared at the curious work of art. "Whatever you do, honey, don't become an artist," was Estrella's advice.

Edelie merely grumbled something and swung the painting on its hinges. It revealed a sizable hole, big enough for a big girl like herself to crawl through. She'd spent many a happy afternoon in there, enjoying the company of some dear friends like Tolkien, Stephen King, and Neil Gaiman, and had come to think of it as her own personal space. Bringing her sisters here felt wrong, somehow, but then there were more important matters to deal with right now than her personal feelings, so she led the way into the wall, Strel and Stien not far behind.

"It's dark in here!" Estrella remarked. "How do you see where you're going?"

"The miracle of electricity," she said dryly and flicked on the lights. A few scattered old lightbulbs flickered to life, and provided scant illumination.

"Are there any spiders in here?" Ernestine asked suspiciously. "Or rats?"

"Spiders? Rats? Where?!" Estrella cried.

"Just follow me," Edelie said morosely, climbing the ladder-like structure hammered into the outer wall. The outer wall was brick, and the inner mainly consisted of plaster on wood with some bricked-up parts. And between the two walls there was a crawling space large enough for a grown person to move around in. Why they'd constructed the house like this she didn't know, but it was way cool, and part of the reason she loved this house so much.

She moved up out of the basement level, and they were now crawling along the hallway. Her favorite spot was the attic, since no one ever went up there, and a small room had been constructed where she liked to curl up with her books whenever she didn't feel like seeing people—which was often.

"How much further is it?" asked Ernestine as she spat out dust. Being the last one, each time her sisters hit a patch, some drywall or splintered wood rained down on her, which, Edelie could imagine, wasn't a lot of fun.

"Almost there," she said, panting a little. The steps that consisted of wooden planks nailed into the wall were worn out, and from time to time she had to press her back against the inner wall while negotiating the steps lest she tumbled down and took the others along with her. Luckily on each floor wooden beams and brick foundation provided a welcome resting spot.

The others joined her, and the threesome took a break from their acrobatics.

"So where's Gran's room?" Ernestine whispered as she tried to peer through the wall.

"Over there," Edelie whispered back and moved to the left, careful where she placed her feet. She glanced through a small crack in the wall and saw they were still in the corridor. She could see the landing and the balustrade. Moving along, she sidestepped some electrical wiring and pointed it out to the others. They didn't want to get electrocuted in here!

Finally, she'd reached Gran's room, and she peered through an opening in the wall. She gasped a little at what she saw. Gran was playing with a pile of diamonds, the biggest one the size of an egg, the smallest ones still the size of a fingertip. And all the while, as she rolled them through her fingers, a small smile was playing about her lips, and she was humming a little tune that sounded eerie to a degree. The worst part? It was a man's voice!

She quickly made way for the others, so they, too, could catch a glimpse of Gran, and they seemed just as startled as she was by this weird person in there who was as far removed from their grandmother as could be.

At least they'd solved one mystery: there was no man in Gran's room, it was Gran herself.

Watching the others watching Gran, her eyes dipped down to the wooden beams that shored up the second floor, and suddenly she saw a mouse, staring back at her with its beady little eyes, nose twitching and whiskers moving!

She almost yelled out, for she was not a mouse person. At all! She wanted to get out of here, right now, but her sisters were in the way. And she couldn't tell them to get a move on either, for on the other side of the flimsy wall—just plaster and wallpaper—some... *creature* was counting its diamonds!

Sweat broke out on her brow and dripped down her face as she was locked in a staring contest with the tiny white mouse.

Then, suddenly, she thought of something. She was a witch, and according to Tavish Mildew a pretty good one, if only she focused her skills on her chosen—or rather unchosen—profession of being a witchy thief. And wasn't getting rid of mice part of a thief's job description? She wasn't a thief yet, but she thought it just might be! So she focused on the mouse, and made a slight gesture with her hand, whispering, "*Disapparato*." There was a soft pop, and the mouse suddenly increased in size, now as big as a chihuahua!

Oh, God, that was so not what she had in mind! She wanted to make the mouse disappear! She made another move with her hand and suddenly the mouse was joined by about a dozen of its colleagues, all staring up at her with curious eyes, and then suddenly more and more mice started pouring from the cracks and fissures in the walls, raining down onto her head and crawling into the neck of her sweater, their tiny feet tickling the bare skin of her back!

With a horrified cry of terror, she lashed out frantically, and stormed forward, bursting through the wall into Gran's room, crashing through like a screaming banshee, the entire mice colony dangling from her hair, her ears, her clothes... "Get them off!" she screeched. "Get them off me!"

Gran, if she was surprised, didn't show it. All she did was quickly tuck away her diamonds and stare at her granddaughter popping in for a visit, bearing gifts in the form of about a thousand mice!

"Edelie!" she cried. "What in heaven's name..."

"I'm sorry, Gran," she yelled as she jumped up on the woman's dresser. "I was passing through and this... bunch of critters decided to join me!"

Gran seemed to enjoy the sudden intrusion, for she grinned widely, displaying a fine set of dentures, and yelled, "Estrella and Ernestine, why don't you join us?!"

The two sisters sheepishly crawled out of the wall. They were as surprised as Edelie to find their grandmother clapping her hands with glee.

"Now that you've managed to destroy this room, I think it's time to finish the job!" the woman yelled. "Ernestine. Estrella. Edelie. Tear out those walls and let's turn this crappy old house into something nice and funky!"

"What do you mean?" Edelie asked from her perch on the dresser. The mice had finally deserted her and were now disappearing back into the wall.

Gran gave her a slightly crazed look. "I'm sick and tired of this ugly old dosshouse and this dreary old room. Let's turn my room into a game room!"

"But Gran!" Ernestine cried. "You can't do this!"

Was it just Edelie's imagination, or had Gran grown a few inches? She seemed to dominate the room, her head almost reaching the ceiling now.

"Turn this room into a game room, Ernestine," bellowed Gran. "That's an order. And when you're done, start on the garden." She ticked off on her fingers. "Pool, Jacuzzi, garage, and add in some old-timers while you're at it."

"Old-timers?"

"Cars, dear. Fill that garage up with cars for your dear old granny!"

"But how are you going to move your cars in and out of the garage?" Estrella pointed out an aspect that had been puzzling Edelie as well.

Gran grinned evilly. "Through the kitchen, of course. Let's do some remodeling while we're at it! Let's turn the downstairs into a driveway and move the kitchen, parlor and living room up to the second floor."

"But where are we going to sleep?" Ernestine asked, wide-eyed.

Gran jerked her thumb up. "On the third floor, of course."

The three sisters gasped at this. The third floor was where Gran's 'office' was, where countless witches over the course of time had made their home and had honed their craft. It was full of bookcases loaded with spell books and witchcraft manuals, all manner of witchy widgets lying around.

"But you can't!" Edelie cried. "That's our heritage!"

Gran's eyes were glittering dangerously, and Edelie now saw that they were black as obsidian. "Watch me," she said, her voice dropping an octave.

Chapter 29

*S*am was going over the evidence again. He'd put pictures of the victims on his computer, and was studying them intently, a hard look on his face. All of them had been beautiful, successful, full of life, and now they were all gone. It was depressing, and even though after years on the force he considered himself a tough son of a gun, he still felt the impact. The invisible choker, he thought grimly as he watched the long procession of grizzly pictures, was one smooth killer. And they had nothing on the guy. Nothing.

Then he noticed Pierre had snuck up on him, moving noiselessly as usual.

"Sam," he said, "I think I might have found something."

A flicker of hope alighted in the back of Sam's mind. "Something?"

"Yeah, I don't know if it's relevant, but..." Pierre hesitated. One of his traits was that he was deferential and unassuming to a degree. People sometimes asked why Sam put up with him, as he rarely spoke, and even then it was in hushed tones. But he liked the guy. He was the opposite of brash and annoying. Quiet, modest, and sweet-natured. And sweet-toothed, of course.

Furthermore, he was quick and efficient and highly conscientious about his work. He was the ultimate administrator, always making sure the paperwork was in order, all the T's crossed and I's dotted. Above all, Sam liked his energy. Self-effacing and easy to get along with.

And sometimes, like now, he managed to take him completely by surprise.

"Show me what you got," he said.

Pierre handed him an old file folder, then shrugged. "Like I said, it's probably nothing."

He stared at the file folder. It was some old murder case from fifteen years ago. But when he studied the file, he immediately noticed the similarities. The woman was beautiful, twenty-five, and successful in her career as an art curator. And she'd been murdered by strangulation, the coroner completely stumped about the murder weapon. Almost as if it was an invisible cord.

He locked eyes with Pierre, who looked almost apologetic. "This guy's been at it for fifteen years?"

In response, Pierre handed him a dozen more files. To his surprise, Sam found they dated back even further, some of them going back forty years!

"This is all I could find, but I'm sure there are more," Pierre said. He tapped the top file. "Ties to the occult. All of them had the coroner stumped. Looks like they're grouped in clusters, every five years or so. Like the guy goes on a killing spree, then lays low for five years before starting again."

Sam's eyes were drawn to a file that listed a double homicide. Twenty years old, involving a man and a woman. When his eyes fell on the names, he did a double take. Abra and Merrill Flummox. "This can't be," he muttered.

Pierre chuckled. "Yeah, I saw that. What are the odds, huh?"

Sam snapped open the file and started to read. Before long, the worry that'd niggled at the back of his mind about the Flummox sisters and their grandmother's association with Ronny Mullarkey increased tenfold. Abra and Merrill hadn't merely been into the supernatural, with Abra allegedly dabbling in witchcraft, but there had been rumors of burglary, though nothing had ever been proven. Merrill Flummox himself had been arrested a few times before he got married. Several counts of B&E, even as a juvie. And now here was this Ronny Mullarkey, also a burglar, and best friends with Cassandra Beadsmore, Abra Flummox's mother... What the heck? He suddenly made a decision and quickly rose from behind the desk.

"I gotta run," he announced, snatching his jacket from the chair.

"Want me to tag along?" Pierre asked.

He eyed the man for all of two seconds, then nodded, and the two cops quickly made their way out of the office. Something fishy was going on, and he'd be damned if he wasn't going to get to the bottom of this ASAP.

Chapter 30

*E*delie watched her grandmother in shock. "You can't destroy the third floor, Gran," she said. "It houses decades of witchcraft—some of it going back to Fallon Safflower herself!"

"Well, time to give it a good cleaning, then," Gran smirked. She was still growing, Edelie saw, and now her head was almost flush with the ceiling. She suddenly stabbed a finger in Ernestine's direction. "You haven't shown me any magic tricks yet, dearie. I'm starting to think you're not a real witch."

"I *am* a real witch," insisted Ernestine, stung to the quick.

"Well, then, why don't you show me?" challenged Gran. "You can start by leveling that ugly greenhouse and putting down a nice big slab of concrete." And with these words, grandmother's head breached the ceiling, and the three sisters watched as she cackled loudly, looking around with glee. "Just like I thought! This place needs a real good cleaning!" she screeched.

Suddenly it started raining spell books and witchy manuals and broomsticks and even the pointy hat that used to belong to Fallon Safflower!

"Gran!" Ernestine yelled. "Stop!"

But Gran wasn't to be deterred, as she kept rooting around,

candles and incense and pentagrams and stuffed toads and glass orbs all raining down.

"She's destroying the house!" Estrella cried.

"We have to stop her!" Edelie added.

The three sisters eyed each other hesitantly. "But how? We're no match for Gran," Ernestine voiced the thought they all shared.

"We have to! She's destroying everything!" Estrella pointed out.

They stared up at the ceiling, where Gran was still rooting around, their heritage crashing down all around them as she seemed to be enjoying herself tremendously, a booming laugh echoing through the house.

As if on cue, the three sisters raised their hands, and shouted out, "*Verisimilinasci!*"

The spell was supposed to show the true nature of a person, and Edelie hoped it would bring out whoever was hiding inside Gran, whether man or beast. Instead, it seemed to tickle the witch, for she tittered loudly.

"That was fun!" she screeched, peering down into the room at the three girls at her feet. "Do it again! Give me more of that delightful witchcraft!"

"*Verisimilinasci!*" the three sisters yelled again, waving their hands just so. And then suddenly it happened: Gran's face simply exploded! Pieces of skin and bone and blood splattered the walls, and instead of Gran's face now suddenly the face of a man appeared. His features were long and ended in an intricately groomed beard that accentuated a cruel thin-lipped mouth, now curled up into a vicious smile, black eyes glittering dangerously.

"Well, well, well. Looks like you three are witches, after all," he said softly, then suddenly reached out a massive hand, trying to snatch them up.

Uttering startled screams, the triplets managed to evade him, however, and disappeared back into the wall, clambering down as fast as they could.

"Who's that?" Ernestine cried.

"That must be Joshua!" Estrella yelled.

"He looks mean!" Edelie added her own two cents. She was bringing up the rear, which was not a good idea, as Joshua's claw-like hand was reaching into the space between the walls, causing big chunks of straw, stucco and brick to rain down on top of her. When he brushed her head, she screamed and lost her balance, slipping and tumbling down on top of her sisters.

"Hey!" Ernestine squeaked when Edelie dropped down on her head.

"Hey!" Estrella squealed when two sisters dropped down on her head.

In a flailing mess of arms and legs, the triplets crashed into the basement, rolled from the hole in the wall, obliterating Edelie's nice black painting, and sat coughing and sputtering for a moment, trying to figure out how many bones they'd broken. Quite miraculously, they discovered, they were still in one piece, and quickly stood and dusted themselves off.

"We have to stop him!" Ernestine said between two coughs. "This Joshua, or whoever he is, is not going to destroy Safflower House!"

"Or us," Edelie added.

"Or Gran," said Estrella.

They stared at each other. It was a thought that hadn't occurred to them. If Gran was Joshua, then where was the real Gran? Or had he taken control of her and their spell had killed her? That was a horrible thing to consider. That their miserable witchcraft might have killed their own grandmother!

"I don't think she's dead," Ernestine finally said.

"How do you know?" Edelie asked miserably.

"I can feel it in my heart," she said, tapping her chest.

The three of them looked much the worse for wear. After their journey through the walls, pieces of plaster were stuck to their hair, and blood streaked their white faces. But in spite of all that, they were determined.

"You're right," said Edelie with a nod. "I can feel her, too."

Estrella was checking her ruined clothes. "So where is she?"

"She can't be far," Ernestine opined.

"Unless that Ronny guy buried her somewhere!" Estrella pointed out.

It was not a very comforting thought.

"Maybe that's why Joshua wants to destroy the garden. Gran is buried somewhere out there!" Edelie added.

"Gran is still alive," Ernestine repeated. "I can feel it. And she's out in the garden somewhere."

"I'll bet she's in the greenhouse!" Edelie suddenly shouted.

"*That's* why he wants me to put a big slab of concrete on top of it! To bury Gran once and for all!" Ernestine agreed.

"We have to find her," Estrella decided. "She's the only one who can stop Joshua."

Then a big piece of plaster fell down from the ceiling, and a loud crashing sound could be heard. "The guy's destroying the whole house!" Edelie cried, and sure enough, just then a foot crashed down into the basement, and the entire ceiling was ripped away, and an evil bearded face appeared.

"Oh, this is where you're all hiding!" he bellowed, and before they could stop him, he plucked Ernestine from their midst and was dragging her away.

Chapter 31

"What do you want with me?" Ernestine protested angrily as the big brute carried her into the garden. She looked over his shoulder and saw that the house had been half demolished by now, her two sisters crawling out of the basement and sneaking over to the greenhouse. She had to buy them some time so they could find Gran and dig her up if she was buried there.

"You haven't shown me any of your powers yet, dear," Joshua said in his best interpretation of Gran's voice. It was eerie to hear Gran's dulcet tones rolling from this monster's lips.

"What did you do to Gran?!" she yelled, helplessly pummeling his leg.

"Oh, no, you don't get to ask the questions around here," he replied in a singsongy voice. He was towering over her, his big feet trampling all over Gran's beloved flower beds and reducing them to patches of wasteland. "You promised me you were going to use your witchy trickery on me, and so far I haven't seen anything yet."

"I destroyed your face, didn't I?"

"Don't take credit for something your sisters did, dear," he drawled. "Now I know those two are witches—real witches—but you?" He shrugged, plunking down and dropping her at his feet. "I don't think you're a witch."

"I *am* a witch," she insisted.

He shook his head languidly. "I think your grandmother was right. Your sisters got all the witch genes, and you were left with nothing."

"Gran said that?" she asked, surprised.

"Yes, she did. She said Edelie and Estrella are the only talented ones in your family. Poor Ernestine is just a hopeless case is what she said." He held up his hand. "Swear to God, those were the exact words she used."

Ernestine was shaking her head. "She didn't say that," she protested feebly. After her shock dismissal from the law firm, this was yet another blow to her self-esteem. She looked up into the warlock's bearded face. "Did she?"

"Afraid she did. Hey, it happens in the best families. Some kids get all the good genes, and some are left with the leftovers. I guess you just got the crap."

"I'm not crap!" she stated adamantly. "I'm a witch, and I can prove it!"

"Don't bust a gut, dear," he said with a chuckle. "I mean, if you haven't got it in you, there's nothing you can do about it. Heck, look at me. I wanted to be blessed with a lot more of those powers than the universe gave me, so I went and got me some. But I realize not everyone is as resourceful as me."

She was going to show this big brute just what kind of a witch she really was! So she raised her hands, pointed at Joshua, and bellowed, "*Bindanatio*!"

But instead of being trussed up like a chicken as she'd intended, the evil warlock merely giggled. "Hey, I felt that! Maybe you're right, maybe you do have some magic in you. Not a lot, though. Why don't you give it another shot? The second time it just might work!"

"Bindanatio!" she yelled again, waving her hands in his general direction.

He checked himself, a comical expression on his face. "I don't know what that was supposed to accomplish, but I'm afraid it didn't work. Just like that little reveal spell you and your sisters tried on me before didn't work. The only reason your gran's face dropped away was because I wanted it to."

She sagged and sat down on the ground. "Oh, crap," she muttered.

"Crap is right," he said, grinning evilly. "That's three for three, dear."

And with these mysterious words, he went into his pocket and brought out a small pouch, then picked out three gems and rolled them in his palm.

"Three stones for three witches," he said, hovering his other hand over them. And as she watched, she saw the three stones change color. One yellow, one blue, one red. "One stone for each of you," Joshua supplied helpfully, "to bind you to my will." And then he flicked his fingers, and the three stones rose up from his hand. And as Ernestine watched helplessly, they all morphed into small radiant hoops, dancing in midair, eager to begin their devastating work. She finally understood. Three hoops to kill three witches!

"You're the invisible choker!"

"Oh, yes, I am," he confirmed. "My stones are very sensitive instruments. They require careful calibration. Just a little bit of your witchcraft is all they need to get your signature and work their own brand of magic." He gave her a wicked grin. "And then it's just a matter of squeezing every last drop of witchiness from your body. Enough to last me another few years. Too bad the process is quite... deadly," he grunted and flung the hoops in her direction.

She rolled to her side, and the hoops missed her, shooting right past her.

"Don't worry, dear," he yelled. "They always get their witch!"

And then she was running toward the greenhouse, the three hoops right behind her, zooming in like cruise missiles honed to her specific signature.

"Strel! Edie! Run!" she shrieked as she exploded into the greenhouse.

Inside, her sisters were digging a hole and looked up in surprise.

"No time!" she screamed as she streaked toward them, and just then the three hoops came crashing through the glass wall of the greenhouse, relentlessly hurtling in their direction.

Edelie and Estrella immediately heaved their shovels and knocked the first two hoops out of course, and Ernestine dove into a bush of gardenias to escape hers. But the things simply streaked past them and then came zooming right back. They simply kept on coming!

Just then, from a corner of her eye, she saw something familiar. In the hole her sisters were digging. A patch of beige she instantly recognized.

"Gran!" she yelled. "Look, it's Gran!"

And as Estrella and Edelie stood sentinel with their shovels, knocking back the hoops, Ernestine stuck her hands in the earth and lay bare Gran's body. Gran's eyes were closed, and she quickly pressed a finger to her throat. Thank God, she was alive! Only now did she see Gran was trussed up with three similar hoops.

"How do I remove them?!" she frantically called out.

She tried to think—to figure out what to do, but they were under attack, and it was hard to focus on anything other than their mere survival.

"Those things probably can't kill Gran because she's too powerful!" Edie shouted as she evaded another attack, hitting the hoops with all her might. "But they must be keeping her unconscious!"

Ernestine tried pulling, but she jumped back, howling in pain. "Those things sting!"

"They're defending themselves," Strel said. "Only magic works!"

And magic was exactly their weak point.

"Let's try that spell Gran taught me to disentangle my headphones!" Edelie suggested. She was the only one who still used earphones with a cord, her two sisters having switched to wireless ones a long time ago.

"*Inbandtwain!*" the three sisters yelled simultaneously.

There was some movement, as the hoops twitched for a moment, trying to figure out what to do, but then they tightened again, locking Gran in.

"Again! *Inbandtwain!*" the three sisters bellowed.

The hoops jerked, as if slapped, but remained tightly fastened.

"Once more!" Estrella cried.

"It's no good. We have to use our hands!" Ernestine said. Which meant they wouldn't be able to defend themselves against the incoming hoops.

Quick as a flash, the three sisters took position around Gran, forming a triangle over her, pointed their hands at their grandmother, and bellowed, "*Inbandtwain!*" This time, they put every last ounce of intention into the spell.

And this time, the hoops twitched, and suddenly seemed to tear themselves away from Gran, twisting this way and that. Unfortunately, the move had left them vulnerable to the other three hoops, which now descended upon them and slung themselves eagerly around their necks.

And in that exact moment, the greenhouse roof caved in, as Joshua crashed his humongous fist through it, showering them with shards of glass.

"Too late!" the warlock cried, as he saw the three witches dropping to the floor, wrestling with the hoops as they fastened themselves around their throats. And as Ernestine felt her air supply blocked off, the hoop tightening viciously, she saw a shadow rising up behind Edelie, growing rapidly. But then her field of vision burst into a fireworks of tiny white stars, and she dropped to the floor, fighting for air... and life.

Chapter 32

*E*delie was the last of the three sisters to lose consciousness, but before she did, she saw that behind Joshua a large shadow was looming. Soon it dwarfed the warlock, and when he finally became aware of the presence of something behind him, it was too late. A bright yellow spark shot from the shadowy figure and drove into his forehead like a spike from a nail gun. And as Joshua fell to earth, his six hoops suddenly disengaged, quickly shrinking back into the colored gems they'd originally been.

The gems rolled over the petunias and the begonias and the rose bushes and tumbled through forsythias until they reached the body of Joshua, who was also shrinking fast now, and then dove into his hand. And as Edelie gasped for breath, she saw that the shadowy giant that had slain Joshua was, in fact, Gran, who was also returning to her own size now, darting a quick glance at Joshua before hurrying over to her granddaughters.

"Oh, Edie, honey!" she gasped, looking a little soiled after having spent all this time buried beneath her own petunias. "Are you all right?"

"The others," she croaked, her voice breaking.

Both she and Gran quickly crouched down next to Estrella

and Ernestine, who were unconscious. "Try a spell, Edelie," Gran said ominously.

"But I'm likely to kill them!" Edelie protested.

"Just try, honey. And have a little faith, will you?"

"*Revitaloh!*" she whispered, intently willing her two sisters to be all right.

And to her intense relief suddenly they both stirred, eyes fluttering open.

"Oh, my darlings," said Gran, hugging Ernestine, then Estrella as they sat up, still dazed.

And then Edelie, too, joined them in their group hug, and then all four of them were crying, but they were tears of relief and happiness, not sadness.

Edelie stared at Joshua, who was still lying prone where he'd fallen.

"Is he... dead?" she asked.

"Not dead," Gran said. "I've merely stripped him of his powers, just like he's stripped so many witches of theirs."

"That's what he was after?" Estrella asked. "Our powers?"

"Yes, he's murdered dozens of witches over the years," Gran said sternly, "feeding on their powers, and he was about to do the same to you three."

"He couldn't kill you, though, could he?" Ernestine asked.

"No, he couldn't. I'm well-protected," Gran said, pointing at her earrings.

Edie stared at them. "Those are the ones we gave you for your birthday."

"Yes," Gran said with a warm smile. "They represent the love of my granddaughters, which is the most powerful protection of all."

"Did he kill our parents?" Estrella now asked.

Gran nodded. "He did. Your mother and father tried to steal his gemstones, the source of his power, but they hadn't counted on the stones being imbued with his personality. The stones turned against them, and strangled them." She shook her head sadly. "If only I'd known what they were up to, but by that point we'd lost touch. I..." She sighed. "Abra and I had a disagreement, and we hadn't spoken to each other in over a year."

"You didn't want Mom to marry Dad, isn't that right?" Edelie asked.

She looked surprised. "How do you know about that?"

Ernestine grinned. "We've been talking to Tavish Mildew. He's been trying to warn us about Joshua."

Gran pursed her lips. "Tavish Mildew. Now there's a name I haven't heard in a while. He was one of your father's friends. A thief and a warlock."

The three girls decided not to take up Tavish's defense. There was still too much they didn't know about the man. Edelie followed Gran's look as she took in the devastation of the house. Their beautiful home was demolished.

"Don't worry," Gran said, pressing their hands tightly. "I can fix that." Then she gave her three granddaughters a cheeky look. "Or maybe you can?"

"Oh, no, Gran!" they all cried simultaneously, and only now did Edelie notice that both her sisters' hair had fallen out and that their faces had suddenly turned... blue. "Um, Gran?" she asked, pointing at her sisters.

"That's just a little side effect, honey. I'm sure it will go away."

Just then, Estrella touched her hair and discovered it was gone. "What... I'm bald!" she bleated. "Gran, I'm bald!"

"Me too!" Ernestine screamed, who'd come to the same conclusion after patting her head. Then she saw her hands, and shrieked, "I'm blue! *Blue*!"

"I'm a Smurf!" Estrella wailed. "I'm Smurfette!"

"I'm bald and I'm *blue*!" Ernestine recapped quite succinctly.

"Oh, dear," Gran muttered. "I guess I'll have to fix the house myself."

Edelie, who'd just weathered the anger of a warlock, didn't feel like weathering the anger of her two sisters and was quickly putting some distance between herself and Strel and Stien, who were now screaming at her to undo the damage she'd done. Trouble was, she was pretty sure that if she tried that she'd only make things worse. Do something that couldn't be fixed!

"Gran! Fix us!" Estrella yelled. "You have to fix us!"

"Yeah, Gran. Make us normal again!" Ernestine put in. "Please!"

"I honestly can't do that, honey," Gran said with a sly smile. "What one witch has wrought, can't be unwrought by a witch of the same blood."

"That can't be true!" Ernestine screeched.

"You just made that up!" Estrella squealed.

Edelie was making her way through the house, adamant to steer clear of her sisters, when suddenly a voice called her name. A deep, masculine voice.

Chapter 33

"Christ!" Sam exclaimed as he ran toward the house. "What the hell happened here?!"

Safflower House was a mess, as if some giant wrecking ball had torn through it. The chimney was sticking out of the front yard, and the third floor had caved in, collapsing on top of the second floor.

Just then, he caught sight of Edelie. "Oh, my God! Are you all right?"

"We had a little accident," Edelie said with remarkable equanimity.

"Did you get hit by an earthquake or a gas explosion or what?!"

"Yeah, something like that," she said with infuriating vagueness.

"Where are your sisters? Are they all right? And your grandmother?"

"They, um..." she turned to stare into the garden, which could now be seen from the front door, the kitchen having been wiped away. Then she turned back to him and gave him a small smile. "They're around."

He straightened. "Look, I need to talk to you. Something came up and—"

"Gran!" Edelie called out, and the woman came shuffling up. Granny looked even worse than the house, Sam thought, as if she'd been buried under a mudslide or something. Dirt was stuck to her face and clothes.

"Are you all right, Mrs. Beadsmore?" he asked solicitously. "Did you call an ambulance?"

"Oh, no, I'm perfectly fine," she said. "Just need to clean myself up a bit."

Now there was an understatement, Sam thought. He didn't get it. The house was destroyed, and here these two acted as if nothing had happened. Then he remembered why he'd come, and he affected the look of a cop who's come bearing bad tidings. "I need to talk to you and your granddaughters, ma'am," he said gravely. They'd stepped into the house, and now he saw that there was a big hole in the hallway, and he could look straight into the basement, where one of those big old furnaces stood. "I think we better talk someplace else, though. This place is gonna collapse any minute now."

"It won't collapse," Granny Beadsmore said decidedly. "Now what did you want to discuss with us, Detective?"

"Well, it's about your daughter, ma'am. New evidence has come to light and, um..." He glanced at Pierre, who stood looking around interestedly, like an archeologist at a particularly fascinating Egyptian dig site. "My colleague has discovered that their killer might still be on the loose."

"The invisible choker," Edelie said, and Sam did a double take.

"That's right. How did you know about that?"

"Oh, I read the papers."

She seemed remarkably unfazed, Sam thought.

"Well, it looks like the MO of your parents' murder twenty years ago shares certain similarities with the most recent string

of murders. And we have reason to believe they're connected."
He eyed the twosome seriously. "Abra and Merrill may well have
been victims of the invisible choker."

"He's here," Edelie suddenly said. "The invisible choker?" she
added when he simply stared at her, too stunned for speech. "We
caught him."

"What!" he cried, finding his voice again. "Why didn't you say
so?!"

"He came after us," Edelie explained. "But we managed to stop
him." She gestured with her head. "He's over in the greenhouse.
Well, what's left of it."

Sam quickly drew his weapon and so did Pierre, but Gran
assured him with a smile, "Oh, you don't have to worry about
him. He's quite harmless. My girls knocked him out before he
had the chance to do any real damage."

"Christ!" Sam barked, and ran into the house, narrowly
avoiding dropping down into the basement, and yelling to Pierre,
"Watch your step!"

The women were right, he soon found. In the middle of the
greenhouse, which was just as a big of a mess as the house itself,
some guy was lying unconscious. He was a big fellow with a
fashionable beard, like Iron Man. Whether he was the invisible
choker or not he did not know, but if Edelie said he'd tried to
attack her and her sisters, that was good enough for him.

"Do you think this is the guy?" Pierre asked, pointing his gun
at the man.

"We'll know soon enough," he said grimly. "Call for backup.
And don't let him out of your sight for one second."

He returned inside and briefly thought he saw Ernestine's
face flashing by. But it couldn't be her, of course, for she was
completely blue, like one of those Avatar creatures. He was

starting to see things. "Mrs. Beadsmore. Miss Flummox," he said when he'd joined the two women again, "I'm going to have to take your statements. And those of Ernestine and Estrella too."

"Of course," said Cassandra courteously. "Do we need to travel with you to the police station, Detective? Or can we do this here and now?"

"Well, I'm afraid you don't have much of a house left to sit down in."

"Yes, that is quite an inconvenience," Cassandra agreed, sharing an odd look with Edelie. "Perhaps we better join you at the police station, then."

"I think that would be for the best. What about Ernestine and Estrella?"

Cassandra's eyes closed momentarily, her lips moving wordlessly, and she seemed to make a little gesture with her hands that made Sam frown. Then she opened her eyes again, and yelled out, "Estrella! Ernestine!"

And to Sam's surprise, the two sisters suddenly emerged, looking a little frazzled but otherwise perfectly fine. And definitely not blue. "You were really lucky, do you know that?" he asked as they stepped from the house.

"Oh, we do know that," said Cassandra. "We are very lucky indeed."

There seemed to be some kind of bad blood between the sisters, for when he turned around, Estrella was pulling Edelie's hair for some reason, and Ernestine was pinching her. Sisters, he thought with a chuckle. He had two sisters himself, and whether they were two or twenty, nothing ever changed.

And as he opened the door to let the women into his car, he told them, "I'll just be a minute," and hurried back into the house. And as he strode in, to his surprise the big hole in the hallway wasn't there anymore, as if the floor had somehow magically repaired itself. He stared at it for a moment, then shook his head. Seeing things, just like before. This case was getting to him.

And when he stepped into the garden, he saw that the killer had regained consciousness, and he was now handcuffed, in spite of his vocal protestations.

"I won't be arrested!" he shouted. "I can't be arrested!"

"Well, then this is a first for you, huh?" Sam shouted back.

"You'll never convict me," the killer taunted, his remarkable black eyes glittering menacingly. "You haven't got a shred of evidence! Nothing!"

"We'll convict you, all right," Sam growled, getting into the guy's face. "We've got eyewitnesses who'll testify you attacked them in their own home."

"No, they won't," he said, staring him down, cool as a cucumber.

"Wanna bet?" he asked, then told Pierre, "Get this guy out of here."

In the distance, police sirens could be heard, backup on approach. It was still a mystery what had happened here, but he was sure the Flummox sisters and their grandmother would paint a complete picture, and then the invisible choker would get what he deserved, the women of this city finally safe again.

Epilogue

*T*he three sisters were seated around the kitchen table, while Gran was cooking up a storm. In celebration of their newly restored house, she'd decided that it was time for her magical pancakes—pancakes with that extra special ingredient that made them extra-yummy. What the ingredient was, Gran had never disclosed. "That's why it's a secret!" she always said.

Edelie thought it was simply better butter in the batter. And more sugar, of course. She was trying to read a book, but was having a hard time focusing, for the TV was blaring in the corner of the kitchen, Gran was happily prattling on about her pancakes, and Strel and Stien were trying to decide how many witches it took to vanquish a warlock. At the moment they agreed on a dozen, which Edelie thought was simply not right.

"It only takes *one* witch to vanquish a warlock, you guys," she finally said with a groan. "Don't you get it? We girls are just as powerful as guys are!"

"So why did it take the four of us to vanquish Joshua?" Ernestine asked.

"Actually it took one witch to vanquish him. Gran," Edelie pointed out. "All we did was make sure she could do her job while we distracted him."

"She's right, you know," said Estrella, studying her newly painted fingernails. "All we did was free Gran so she could take care of Joshua."

"So then why isn't he dead? If it only takes one witch to destroy a warlock, why is Joshua in jail right now and not, you know, gone?"

Edelie's attention was drawn to the television, where Sam Barkley was just being interviewed. "Um, you guys? I think you should see this."

Estrella turned up the volume, and the threesome stared at the screen, where Sam stood defending himself against an irate crowd in front of the police station. Apparently Joshua had just walked from jail, free as a bird, the NYPD incapable of keeping him locked up for lack of evidence.

"Where are the witnesses?" a CNN reporter was yelling. "I thought you said you had eyewitnesses to the invisible choker's crimes? Where are they?"

Sam was looking extremely agitated, and Edelie couldn't blame him. Joshua walking was a big embarrassment to his department. "They backed out at the last minute. Seems like the whole thing was just one big mistake."

The three sisters turned to Gran, aghast. "Gran!" cried Ernestine. "You didn't!"

Gran shrugged. "I can't very well tell the police that we're witches and that we were attacked by a warlock, can I? Joshua threatened to expose us."

They'd gone into the station where Sam had questioned them, and Edelie had discovered it was very hard to say anything without compromising themselves. They couldn't tell the police that Joshua had taken the place of Gran. They couldn't tell them he destroyed the house by growing as big as the house itself. They couldn't talk about the gemstones and their mystical powers and how he used them to kill witches. And they certainly couldn't tell them Gran had vanquished him by knocking him out with one of her spells!

So in the end the only thing she'd told Sam was that Joshua had dropped by the house that night and had threatened to kill them and that they'd jumped him and subdued him. Sam was disappointed, and seemed to feel they were holding back. He wanted to know why the house was demolished, and when she told him it was a gas explosion, he slammed the table and said Gran had told him it was an earthquake—miraculously ignoring all the other houses on the block—that Estrella said a tornado had struck out of the blue and Ernestine thought it was a meteor that had crashed through the roof.

No, it was safe to say Sam Barkley wasn't their biggest fan right now, but to let Joshua walk like this? That was insane!

"He can't do anybody any harm," Gran pointed out as she placed the plate with pancakes on the table. "I took away his powers, remember?"

"All he needs to regain them is to murder another witch!" Estrella pointed out, and to this Gran didn't seem to have an answer, for she merely smiled.

And they'd just dug in, the four of them—though Estrella said she really shouldn't, considering the diet she was on—when the doorbell rang.

"Oh, I'll get it," Edelie grumbled when the others simply ignored it. She loved pancakes, and she hoped her sisters wouldn't devour the entire stack.

Before she left the kitchen, she caught Gran's eye, and saw that that same smile was still firmly in place. A little puzzled, she sauntered off.

She slouched through the hallway, then opened the door with a sigh, fully expecting it to be the UPS guy again, carrying yet another package for Strel. She'd become addicted to the Home Shopping Network lately, buying up widgets by the dozen. But when she opened the door, the first thing she saw was that funky little Iron Man beard, and then those intensely black eyes.

Before she could slam the door shut, she was punched in the chest by the imposing warlock and was flung back several feet, landing on Gran's new Persian rug. Gasping for breath, she cried out, "Joshua! He's back!"

The evil warlock stepped inside, towering over her with a vicious grin on his face. "I have some unfinished business here," he sneered as he took a whiff. "Mh. Pancakes. My favorite. Well, apart from the smell of dead witches, of course." And when Estrella and Ernestine came rushing in from the kitchen, he smirked. "Oh, there you are. Like I told your chubby sister, I seem to have mislaid something." He brought a finger to his lips in mock contemplation. "Oh, yes. My powers!"

And at this, he strew a string of small gemstones from his fingers. They rolled across the floor in Edelie's direction, and before she could scramble to her feet, they were circling her, and then they were up in the air around her, whirling at dizzying speed, turning into the deadly hoops she knew so well. And with every revolution, they seemed to grow bigger and deadlier.

"But Gran took away your powers!" she shouted.

He grinned. "Yes, she did. But my gems only need the tiniest little bit of witchiness to get them going again. What little you have, my dear Edelie, is plenty. More than enough to take you out, and restore my powers in full."

"That's not gonna happen," Edelie grunted, raising her hands. She was sick and tired of this guy.

"You killed our parents!" Estrella yelled.

"You don't deserve to live!" Ernestine added.

Joshua laughed. "Oh, the three little witches are giving me lip? Well, without your granny you're not as powerful as you think you are." And with a flick of the hand, he sent the hoops whirling and attaching themselves to the three sisters' throats, beginning their vile work of choking them.

But the triplets were finally done with the creep.

"*Hvirfillia*!" they all shouted simultaneously, pointing their hands at the warlock. It was an old spell Gran had taught them a long time ago, to make their crib mobiles spin faster or in different directions. They wanted to make this guy's head spin so fast he'd think twice about coming back here.

Joshua was still laughing, his arms outstretched as he soaked up the witching powers of the Flummox triplets. But then, suddenly, his smile disappeared, as first his head started spinning, just like his own hoops, then his neck, and finally his torso and his legs. Parts of his body were all spinning at different velocities, as the three sisters' spells were highly uncoordinated.

And then their coordination broke down completely, as his head spun to the right, his torso to the left, and his legs to the right again, with all his joints spinning in yet different directions still, and at different speeds. The warlock's entire body seemed completely out of control now.

"Hey!" he cried, sounding a little garbled. "Stop that!"

But the three sisters didn't let up, and as they kept repeating '*Hvirfillia*!' under their breaths, their hands kept whirling, tiny colorful sparks now flying from their fingertips and joining the weird dance in front of them.

It was working, for Edelie felt the chokehold of the hoop around her neck finally easing up, and then dropping away completely, as the hoop lost its power and dropped at her feet. Then, just as suddenly, all the hoops zoomed back to their master and joined the frantic dance of whirling body parts.

And even as Edelie rose to her feet, and the three sisters now stood side by side, the warlock disappeared in a cloud of crazily vibrating colors and lights, smoke rising up as if from a clockwork whose parts are spinning into oblivion. Then there was an enormous bang, and when the smoke finally cleared, the warlock was gone! A bunch of marbles dropped to the floor, before they themselves also popped, one by one, and vanished into thin air. Soon, nothing was left of Joshua but a small greenish stain on the rug.

"Nothing Mr. Clean can't fix," Edelie said with a satisfied nod.

Just then, Gran walked out of the kitchen, a stern look on her face. "Girls! Your pancakes are getting cold!" Then she threw one look at the green stain, and muttered, "Need to clean that up." And with a minute gesture of her head and a whispered spell, the stain suddenly vanished with a soft crumpling sound, and Joshua, the invisible choker, was gone for good.

Gran eyed the three of them intently for a moment, then a warm smile lit up her gentle features, and she gave them a knowing nod, as if to say, 'You guys did good.' When she disappeared into the kitchen again, she was muttering something about stains, as if none of this had ever happened.

The three sisters shared a proud grin. They might not be the greatest witches in the world, and every single one of their spells backfired quite disastrously, but they'd still managed to vanquish their first warlock.

And as Edelie glanced around the hallway, which was now back the way it was before the intrusion of Joshua, as was the rest of the house and garden, she felt a sudden and very

---

uncharacteristic surge of happiness bubbling up inside of her. For the first time in years, she felt she actually had a purpose in life. Something uniquely hers. And as she stared at her fingers, she saw they were still sparkling softly. And as she watched, the sparkle briefly flared up, then danced from her fingers and across the hall, soon joined by the sparkles of her sisters. The yellow, blue and red twinkles playfully leaped into the picture frame of their parents, hung next to the hallway mirror.

And as the threesome watched in fascination, the sparkles reached their parents' eyes, and a soft but distinct whisper could be heard. "*Witchy fingers!*"

And when Edelie looked at her two sisters, she could tell they'd heard it, too, for they grinned just as wickedly as she did. Whether Gran liked it or not, her three girls were blessed with witchy fingers. On this, the eve of their twenty-first birthday, they'd finally discovered their purpose, and it wasn't singing, or cooking, or lawyering. It was thieving, like only witches can...

Excerpt from Between a Ghost and a Spooky Place

Chapter One

"*I* didn't think you'd show up," the gruff voice announced. Harry looked up from her perusal of the latest James Patterson. She quickly closed the book and shoved it into her backpack, then rose from her perch on the low wall of the underpass. She shrugged as she approached the hulking figure. "I'm always true to my word," she told the man, doing her best not to look or sound intimidated.

He really was a giant of a man, though she'd been told he wasn't as dangerous as he looked. He could have fooled her, though. He had no neck to speak of, his arms alone were probably as thick as her waist, and she could have fitted several times in the long black overcoat he was wearing, she herself being rather on the petite side.

She pushed her blond tresses from her brow and fixed her golden eyes on the stranger, rubbing her hands to keep warm. She'd removed her gloves and knitted cap and now thought perhaps she shouldn't have. The cold drizzle that had started overnight had turned into a real downpour, and even though they were protected from the brunt of the autumn weather by the underpass, the wet cold still crept in Harry's clothes and chilled her to the bone.

"Let's do this," the man grumbled. "I haven't got all day."

The watery sun that had tried to pierce the dark deck of clouds that afternoon had finally given up its struggle, giving free rein to the driving rain. But then this was London, a city that for some reason had collectively decided the sun had no business here, except on those very rare occasions.

She quickly unzipped the main compartment of her backpack and took out the package, then handed it to the client. Through the clear plastic protective cover it was easy to make out its contents, but the burly man insisted on taking the book out nonetheless.

"You're going to get it all smudged," Harry murmured, though she knew this was none of her business. Once the transaction was made, the book belonged to the client, to do with as they pleased, whether she liked it or not.

"Looking good," the man muttered, flipping through the pages of the voluminous tome. "How do I know it's the real deal?"

"You have Sir Buckley's word," she said with a light shrug.

The client scrutinized her carefully, shoving the book back into its plastic covering. Then he nodded once. "Good enough for me," he announced. He handed her a small black briefcase. "One million. As agreed," he told her.

She balanced the briefcase on her knee and clicked it open. Two thousand 500 pound notes should be there and as far as she could determine they were all present and accounted for. But then again, she didn't think the client was going to cheat her. And even if he did, Buckley would handle it.

So she clasped the briefcase under her arm and looked up at the man, a little trepidatious. Buckley had always told her to conclude the meeting the moment the transfer was done, and only rarely did a client linger. This one still stood staring at her, however, as if their business wasn't concluded yet. They were the only two people there, as the underpass was quite deserted.

This was Buckley's favorite place to make a transfer, as this particular spot wasn't covered by any of London's half a million cameras. Which also meant that if a client decided to get any funny ideas, Harry had no recourse. It wasn't as if she had a black belt in jujitsu or some other martial arts discipline. She'd recently watched a video on the Daily Mail website on how to protect yourself against an attack, but hadn't the foggiest notion how to execute those nifty self-defense moves in real life.

The man gave her an unexpected grin, displaying two gold teeth. It was something you didn't see that often these days, and she found herself staring at the shiny snappers before she could stop herself. Along with his bald dome, it gave him the aspect of an old-fashioned James Bond bad guy. But then his smile suddenly disappeared, and he gave her a curt nod. "I guess that concludes our business," he grunted.

"Yeah, I guess it does," she returned.

He abruptly flipped his hoodie over his head, then turned and walked away. Soon he was swallowed up by the shadows stretching long tendrils of darkness beneath the overpass. Moments later she heard a motorcycle kicking into gear, and then its roar as it raced away into the falling dusk.

She heaved a sigh of relief. These exchanges were going to be the death of her one day, she thought as she hurried out of the underpass, to where she'd fastened her bicycle to a streetlight. Fortunately, it was still where she'd left it. She tried to fit the entire suitcase into her backpack but failed, so she tipped its precious contents into her trusty Jack Wolfskin rucksack and dumped the suitcase in a nearby trashcan. And as she adjusted the straps, she noted a little giddily she'd never worn a million pounds on her back before. Then she pressed her pink knitted cap to her head, used her gloves to wipe that fabled London precipitation from her saddle, mounted the bike and was off.

Five minutes later she was pedaling down Newport Street, anxious to get back to the store. She'd only feel at ease once the money was safely transferred to Sir Geoffrey Buckley's cash register. And as she waited for the traffic light to turn green, she idly wondered what she would do with so much money. She could quit her job, buy herself a great house and take that trip around the world she'd been dreaming of for ages. The lights changed, and traffic was off and so was she, stomping down on her silly daydreams. The money wasn't hers and never would be. She was, after all, only a lowly wage slave in Sir Buckley's employ. Why there was a Sir in front of his name, she didn't know, even after working for the man for close to a year now.

Buckley Antiques, the store where she spent her days when her employer wasn't sending her to dark and creepy places to exchange packages with obscure and dangerous-looking clients, was a smallish shop tucked away in the more dingy part of Notting Hill. It carried rare antiques and other items for the connoisseur, its owner and proprietor, the eponymous Sir Geoffrey, priding himself in his capacity to obtain items for his clients that no other antiquarian could find. There was a whiff of the illegal and the criminal attached to both the man and the shop, and oftentimes Harry wondered where he obtained these rare and exclusive items if not by illicit means.

She'd never asked, and Buckley had never told her, of course. She merely did as she was told, and delivered million pound books to men with no necks without asking pesky questions. Such as: why would anyone buy a book for such an incredible price? And why not transfer the items at the store? She didn't ask because she was afraid she wouldn't particularly like the answer.

She couldn't help wonder, though, where the priceless tome would end up, for No-Neck, like Harry herself, was probably only the messenger.

But even though Harry knew that her employer was something of a high-end fence, her conscience was no match for her need of a regular paycheck.

With her history degree she didn't stand much of a chance to find a decent-paying job in London, or anywhere else in the United Kingdom for that matter, and she knew she should be grateful to have found a job at all that was a cut above being a waitress, cleaning lady or nanny. The job might not be completely on the up and up, but it was better than being on welfare.

Besides, for her discretion Buckley paid her a nice little stipend around the holidays, so there was that as well.

She attached her bike to the lantern in front of the store, and entered the shop, her trusty backpack burning with the money. As she stepped inside, the doorbell jangled merrily. As usual, the store was dimly lit, Buckley's way of adding atmosphere. She picked her way past the antique cupboards and Louis XIV armoires and tried to ignore the quite horrendous oil paintings adorning the walls. When she reached the counter, fully expecting to find Buckley pottering about, she was surprised to see him absent from the scene.

No sound could be heard, either, except for the ticking of a dozen antique Swiss cuckoo clocks Buckley had obtained from a Swiss traveling cuckoo clock salesman. A real bargain, he'd called them, though Harry failed to understand who'd ever want to pay good money for such monstrosities.

"Buckley?" she called out. "Buckley, I'm back!"

Usually the prospect of money brought out her employer like the genie from the bottle, but no frizzy-haired elderly gentleman popped up now.

Harry shrugged, and started transferring the money from her backpack to the cash register, which had a deep and convenient space beneath the money drawer. Here it would be quite safe until Buckley put it in the ancient but very sturdy vault he kept in his office.

She wondered briefly if she shouldn't close up the shop, as she wasn't even supposed to be working today. Buckley had called her in to deal with this urgent delivery, and she'd grudgingly complied. He didn't like to deal with his 'special clients' himself, reserving that particular privilege for her.

And it was as she stood wondering what to do when she became aware of a soft groaning sound coming from deeper into the shop. It seemed to come from the back. With a slight swing in her step, relieved to be rid of the huge pile of money, she decided to take a look. She didn't like to lock the door without Buckley's say-so. He had this thing about wanting the store to be open at all hours, even if that meant she had to take her lunch break in between serving customers. But she didn't like to leave it unattended either.

She would just have a look around and as soon as she'd found her employer—probably messing about somewhere in his office— she'd go home. After riding around in the rain for the past half hour she was wet, tired and numb, and a hot shower and some dry clothes looked pretty good right now.

Besides, she needed to put in some shopping and wanted to get it done before rush hour, hoping to salvage what little she could from her day off.

"Buckley?" she called out as she moved deeper into the store. Behind the showroom were two smaller rooms. One was Buckley's office, where he liked to meet with clients and suppliers, and the other was the small kitchen reserved for personnel—which meant her. It wasn't much. Just a table, some chairs, a sink, gas stove and fridge. Next to the kitchen a staircase led upstairs, to the apartment Buckley rented out for a stipend. In exchange, the man, who was rarely in during the day, kept an eye on the store after six.

"Buckley?" she tried again. She noticed that the door to his office was ajar, so she pushed it open. And that's when she saw her employer. He was stretched out on the floor, his limbs arranged in an awkward pose, blood pooling around his head. She clasped a hand to her face, her throat closed on a silent scream, and looked down at the lifeless body. It was obvious she was too late. His eyes were open and staring into space, his face pale as a sheet.

"Oh, Buckley, Buckley," she finally whispered hoarsely, automatically taking her phone from her pocket with quaking hand and dialing 999.

Minutes later, the store was abuzz with police and medics, as she sat nursing a cup of tea in the kitchen, stunned and fighting waves of nausea.

She looked up when she became aware of being watched, and she saw a man looking down at her from the entrance to the kitchen. He was tall and broad and easily filled the doorframe, both in width and height. She noted to her surprise that he was gazing at her with a scowl on his handsome face. Perfectly coiffed dark hair, steely gray eyes, chiseled features and an anvil jaw lent him classic good looks, and for a moment she thought none other than David Gandy himself had wandered into the store, mistaking it for the scene of his latest swimwear shoot. But then the man cleared his throat.

"Inspector Watley. Can I ask you a few questions, Miss McCabre?"

She nodded, wiping a tear from her eye. "Yes, of course, Inspector."

The inspector took a seat at the table and placed a small notebook in front of him, checking it briefly. "Your name is Henrietta McCabre?"

"Yes, but most people just call me Harry," she said softly.

"You were the one who found the body, Miss McCabre?"

"Yes, I did," she said, tears once again brimming in her eyes.

"And what time was this?"

"Must have been... around four. I'd just come back from an errand."

He gave her a dark look. "An errand connected to the store?"

She nodded again. She was loathe to reveal the nature of her errand. Even dead, she didn't want to betray Buckley's confidence.

"Tell me exactly what you saw," Inspector Watley said gruffly.

She quickly told him what had happened, and didn't forget to mention the groan she'd heard—the sound which had alerted her of Buckley's presence.

Watley's frown deepened. "You heard a groan, you say?"

"Yes, I did. It's the reason I came back here. I thought Mr. Buckley had stepped out of the store, as he didn't respond when I called out. So when I heard the groan, I went looking for him... And that's when I found him."

"That's odd," the inspector said, fixing her with an intent stare.

"What is?"

"The groan."

"Why odd? It is perfectly natural for someone who's just tumbled and knocked his head to groan. I'm just surprised I didn't hear it sooner."

"According to the preliminary findings of our coroner, Mr. Buckley must have been dead for at least half an hour before you arrived, Miss McCabre."

This news startled her. "He was dead... before I arrived?"

"Yes, he was."

"Oh, poor Mr. Buckley," she said. "To think he'd been lying there all this time before I found him! If only I'd arrived sooner, he could've been saved." She looked at the policeman. "I knew this would happen. I just knew it."

He stared at her blankly. "You knew he was going to die?"

She nodded. "He was very unsteady on his feet lately. Only last month he took quite a tumble when he stepped from the store. I told him he should get a cane, but he was far too proud." She shook her head, extremely distraught. "It was only a matter of time before he took a bad fall and hit his head."

The policeman eyed her curiously for a moment, then lowered his head and said slowly, "Your employer didn't hit his head, Miss McCabre."

"What do you mean? If he didn't hit his head, then how did he die?"

"Mr. Buckley was murdered, Miss McCabre. Murdered in cold blood with a blunt object by the looks of things." Then, without waiting a beat, he went on, "Can you account for your whereabouts between the hours of three and four, Miss McCabre?"

Her jaw dropped. Was he accusing her of murdering her own boss? "Well, I wasn't here if that's what you mean," she was quick to point out.

"Where were you then?"

And she was about to respond when she remembered she couldn't. Even though providing herself with an alibi was more important than respecting Mr. Buckley's wishes, she still couldn't tell the inspector where she'd been. Not if she didn't want to get in big trouble with No-Neck and his employer.

Chapter Two

*I*t didn't take a genius to figure out she was in a pickle. Not only didn't she have an alibi, but apparently the safe was empty, all of Mr. Buckley's possessions stolen. It was obvious how things looked from Scotland Yard's point of view. They probably figured she'd burgled the safe, seeing as she knew the combination, was caught in the act by her employer, at which point a violent struggle had ensued and she'd violently slain the older man. The only reason she wasn't being placed under arrest was that she'd be an idiot to stick around after the murder, or to call the police herself.

These and other thoughts were now swirling in Harry's head as Inspector Watley told her tersely to please remain available for questioning—probably the Scotland Yard equivalent for 'Don't leave town!'

She nodded quickly, her face now completely devoid of color and her extremities of blood, and wobbly got to her feet the minute Watley left.

And as she made her way out of the store, which was still swarming with police, she feebly wondered what she was going to do now. For one thing, she was most definitely out of a job. Which was something she should have told Watley, she now saw. Clearly she had no motive for murder; it simply meant unemployment. Then again, she'd just tucked a million pounds of motive into the shop till, and who knew how much more money Buckley kept in his safe, along with countless other valuables? Plenty of motive there.

As she rode her bicycle home, the rain was coming down

again in sheets, and even before she'd reached the street where she lived, she was soaked to the skin. A fitting ending to a lousy day, she thought miserably.

Arriving home at Valentine Street No. 9, she quickly fastened her bike to the cellar window grille, wiped the rain from her eyes, and jogged up the steps to the front door. Letting herself in, she stood leaking rainwater on the black and white checkered floor for a moment, then slammed the heavy door shut, and quickly checked the mailbox. A magazine had arrived—the historical magazine she subscribed to—and a bill from the electric company, probably announcing another rate hike.

She hurried up the stairs, already shucking off her jacket, and when she arrived on the landing wasn't surprised to find her neighbor patiently awaiting her arrival, Harry's snowy white Persian in her arms.

"Oh, shoot," she said, taking the cat from the elderly lady. "Did Snuggles sneak into your flat again, Mrs. Peak? I thought I locked her up this time."

Mrs. Peak, the wizened old prune-faced lady who lived next door, gave her a wistful smile. "I don't mind, Harry. I only wish she visited me more often. I wouldn't mind having a darling like Snuggles myself, you know."

"Perhaps one day you will," said Harry as she pulled Snuggles's ear. "If she keeps this up, I just might have to give her away."

Mrs. Peak didn't seem to mind one bit. "Snuggles can drop by any time," she assured her.

"Thank you, Mrs. Peak," she said, letting herself into her flat. And as she closed the door, she whispered, "What's the matter with you, little one? Why do you keep sneaking off to the neighbors, huh? Don't you like it here?"

She put the cat down on the floor and looked around

her modest flat. It wasn't even a flat, really, more of a studio apartment. One living room with kitchenette, a small bedroom, and an even smaller bathroom. Just enough for the student she'd been when she took it, and currently all she could afford on her meager earnings. She'd told herself back then that once she got her first paycheck she was going to find something bigger. But then she'd seen the paltry sum on her paycheck and had realized that it would be a long time before she'd be able to afford anything more than what she had. In fact she was lucky to have a place as nice as this one, London quickly becoming too costly for anyone without a millionaire mum or dad to foot the bill.

She watched as Snuggles haughtily stalked to the window, which was open to a crack, hopped out onto the small balcony, and started to make her way over to Mrs. Peak again. Harry quickly hurried after her and managed to snatch her just before she hopped from her balcony to the next.

"What's wrong with you?" she asked as she took the cat indoors again and closed the window. "Do you get special treats next door? Is that it?"

She checked Snuggles's bowl, but it was still filled to capacity. Possibly she was simply bored with the same dry food and needed something fresh?

And she was just scooping some canned food into a second bowl, much to Snuggles's delight, when she remembered she'd scheduled a call with her cousin.

She hurried over to her laptop, flipped it open and switched it on. And as she made herself a jam sandwich and carried it on a plate to the laptop, she kicked off her soggy sneakers, then hopped into the bedroom to change into something dry. She was just wrapping a towel around her head when the telltale sound of Skype warned her that Alice was online and calling her.

Video image of her cousin flickered to life, and she gave her a jolly wave.

"Hey, honey," Alice said. "Did you just step out of the shower?"

"No, I just stepped out of London, which is basically the same thing."

Alice laughed. She was a perky blonde with remarkable green eyes, and perennially in a good mood. "You should come and visit, Harry. It's about eighty degrees out here and not a single cloud in sight."

Harry sighed. "That sounds like heaven. I wish I could, but…"

"The antique shop, huh? Too much work? I can relate, honey. I'm actually holding down three jobs right now if you can believe it. The mortuary, the gun store, *and* the bakery. Never worked so hard in my life!" Harry nodded absently, and Alice's face fell. "Are you all right? You look very pale."

She shook her head. "Something horrible happened to me today, Alice."

She proceeded to tell her cousin about the murder of her boss, and Alice cried, "Oh, no! You must have been terrified! How are you holding up?"

"I'm… fine, actually. Though at the moment I seem to be the only suspect the police have." She tucked a leg beneath her and told Alice the whole story.

She and her cousin had no secrets from each other. They'd always been close, ever since Alice's father, Curtis Whitehouse, had been stationed in London, working at Scotland Yard in an advisory capacity for five years. Since Uncle Curtis and Aunt Demitria had lived right next door to Harry's parents, she and Alice had been like sisters. The bond had never been broken, even now, when they were thousands of miles apart.

"So they think you have something to do with the murder?"

"Judging from the look on Inspector Watley's face, yes. And I can't even give him an alibi, as my client would never forgive me."

"Who is he?"

She shrugged. "Probably some rich businessman who doesn't want to pay full price for his works of art. Most of them are, Buckley once told me."

"Can't you ask? This No-Neck person must be traceable, right?"

"Actually I have no idea how to get in touch with him. Buckley always made all the arrangements. I just had to show up to make the exchange."

"If I were you I'd try to find the guy," Alice suggested. "Otherwise you're in big trouble, honey. The police will be very suspicious if you won't tell them where you were." She shook her head. "Oh, how I wish I could help you."

She didn't see how she could, though. Even though Alice's father was now chief of police in the small town where he and his family lived, he had no clout with Scotland Yard. Unless...

"Does your father still keep in touch with his old colleagues?"

"He might," Alice admitted. "Do you want me to ask him?"

"Could you? Perhaps if I can just talk to someone, I can explain what happened without betraying the client's confidence."

"All right. Sit tight, hon. I'll give him a call now." Then she paused, looking thoughtful. "You know? There's actually someone else who might be able to help you."

Harry took a bite from her sandwich. She suddenly found she was starving. "There is? Who?"

"He's, um..." Alice bit her lip. "He's a guy who knows people, you know."

"Yes?"

Alice stared at her for a beat. "I'll have to discuss it with him first, though."

"Okay," she said, a little puzzled. It wasn't like Alice to suddenly go all mysterious on her. "Is he from England?"

"No, he's American, but he might know someone over there who can help you." She eyed her anxiously. "I worry about you. You're all alone out there."

"I'll be fine," she said, though she realized that she didn't sound very convincing. It was true that she was quite alone out here. Her parents had died in a car crash the day of her graduation, and since she didn't have any sisters or brothers she basically had to rely on herself. She had an aunt and uncle up in Scotland but hadn't heard from them in ages. The only family she kept in touch with was Alice, which was at least something to be thankful for.

Alice seemed to make up her mind. "I'm going to talk to Brian. I'm going to ask him to pull a few strings."

"Oh, okay," she said. "Who's Brian?"

Alice closed her lips, her face turning red. "I, um, didn't I mention him?"

"No, you didn't." She laughed. "What? Is he, like, your new boyfriend or something?"

"No, of course not! Reece and I are still very much together. You know that."

Alice was engaged to Reece Hudson, a famous movie star. Even Harry had seen a couple of his movies. He was a great guy and loved to goof around with Harry when he and Alice came to London. The couple usually stayed at the Ritz-Carlton, just about the swankiest place Harry had ever seen. Reece wasn't impressed, though. Said he'd stayed in far more luxurious hotels in other parts of the world. Which just went to show how the other half lived.

"Look, I've gotta go," Alice suddenly said.

All this talk about this mysterious Brian had apparently made her nervous, for she flinched when Harry protested, "You still haven't told me who this Brian guy is."

"I'll tell you all about him, honey. But first I need to get him to agree to something." She gave her a long look before asking her the most outrageous question of all. "Do you still... see things, Harry?"

She frowned. "See things? What do you mean? What things?"

"You know. When we were kids, sometimes you used to tell me you saw people who weren't really there, remember? Like... dead people?"

She laughed. "Come on, Alice. You know that was just my overactive imagination."

"No, but you said you saw Gran, remember? You even talked to her."

She did remember, though only vaguely. It was true that when her and Alice's grandmother had passed away, she'd imagined seeing her, after she had supposedly passed on. The old lady had visited ten-year-old Harry's bedroom the night she died. She'd told her that everything would be fine, and that she was moving on to a different plane but that she'd always watch over her and Alice. Later she'd begun to think she'd imagined the whole thing.

"You know that was just a dream," she told her cousin, but Alice didn't seem convinced. "I mean, what else could it have been, right?"

A slight smile played about her cousin's lips, but then she nodded. "Yeah, probably a dream. Anyway, I've got to go."

"Let me know what your father has to say, all right? I really hope he knows someone on this side I can talk to."

"Will do, honey. Love you! Bye-bye!"

She rang off and stared out the window for a while. The rain was lashing the single pane, and the sky was pitch black, even though it wasn't even fully evening yet. Snuggles jumped on her lap and installed herself there, purring contentedly. She stroked her behind the ears. "So it was the food, huh?" she murmured as she settled back.

She thought about what Alice had said about Brian, and wondered what that was all about. But then she figured it had nothing to do with her, and decided not to expect too much. Alice had a habit of making a lot of promises before promptly forgetting all about them. And seeing as she was so busy, it would be a small miracle if she even remembered to ask her father about his Scotland Yard contacts. If he still had any left. It'd been almost ten years since he'd returned to the States and became Happy Bays's chief of police.

She thought back to Inspector Watley, and the dark looks he'd given her. It was obvious that if it were up to him, he'd have arrested her on the spot.

She heaved a deep sigh. "We're in deep trouble, Snuggles," she murmured. "If things don't look up it's not such a bad idea to head on over to Mrs. Peak for your kibble. She might just be your new owner from now on."

She shivered and moved over to the window to close the curtains. For the first time in a long time she didn't have anywhere to be the next day.

Chapter Three

*J*arrett Zephyr-Thornton III was perfecting his ice skating technique when his personal valet beckoned him from the side of the rink. As per his instructions, the rink had been closed off to the public to allow Jarrett to practice in private. It was his dream to become the next big thing in figure skating, and since he'd never been on the skates before, but he'd seen all the movies, he knew that practice made perfect, so practice it was.

He was a spindly young man with wavy butter-colored hair and pale blue eyes that regarded the world with child-like wonder. As the son of the richest man in England he was in the unique position to do whatever he wanted whenever he wanted to do it, and what he wanted more than anything right now was to be the next British figure skating Olympic champion.

He groaned in annoyance when he caught sight of his valet Deshawn's urgent wave. "I told you to hold all my calls!" he cried, but the music pounding from the speakers drowned out his voice. It was the soundtrack of *Ice Princess*, of course, playing on a loop. Motivation was key, he knew, and he watched the movie at least once a day to keep him in the right frame of mind.

Reluctantly he finished his pirouette and swished over to the side.

"Yes, yes, yes," he grumbled when Deshawn handed him the phone. "This is Jarrett!" he called out pleasantly when it was finally pressed to his ear. "Oh, it's you, Father," he said with an exaggerated eye roll. "What am I doing?" He frowned at Deshawn, who shrugged. Father never asked him what he was doing. Just as Jarrett made it his aim in life to do as little as possible, his pater made it his habit to interfere as infrequently as possible, lest he develop a heart condition. "I'm ice skating, if you must know," he said a little huffily, fully expecting a barrage of criticism to be poured into his ear at this confession. "For what? The Olympic Games, of course. What else?"

"Look, son, something's come up," the author of his being now grated in his ear. "I need you to listen to me and listen to me very carefully, you hear?"

He did listen very carefully, even though he was quite sure that whatever the old man had to impart was probably a load of poppycock as usual. "Yes, Father. I am listening," he announced with another eye roll. There was a crackling noise on the other end, and then his father said, "I need you or that valet of yours to go over to..." There was that crackle again.

"There seems to be some sort of noise. What did you just say?"

"I need you to pick up the parcel and bring it to..."

"I'm losing you," he said, quickly losing patience.

"The parcel is at... right now, and if you don't pick it up... it's going to... along with your mother's... and that'll be the end of..."

"You're not making any sense," he said, staring down at his nice new blue spandex outfit. He'd bought seven, a different color for each day of the week. He particularly liked the one he was wearing now. It looked exactly like the one Michelle Trachtenberg, the star of *Ice Princess*, wore in the movie. "What package? And what does Mother have to do with anything?"

"Will you just listen!" the old man yelled, now audibly irritated. "If you don't pick up that package right now... then... and... unmitigated disaster!"

He sighed. Whatever his old man was involved in, it could probably wait, so he said, "First get decent reception, Father, and call me back, all right?"

And he deftly clicked off the phone and handed it back to Deshawn. He then gave his valet a look of warning. "No more phone calls, Deshawn."

Deshawn, a rather thickset smallish man with perfectly coiffed thinning brown hair and an obsequious manner, had been in Jarrett's employ for many years, and the two formed rather an odd couple. One thin and tall, the other short and stout, they resembled Laurel & Hardy in their heyday.

The valet now muttered, "I know, sir. My apologies. But your father said it was extremely urgent."

"It's always urgent," said Jarrett with an airy wave of the hand. "But he'll just have to wait, for I..." He glided away. "... am on my way to greatness!"

And with these words, he allowed the wonderful music of *Ice Princess* to guide him back onto the rink and launch him into his most complicated movement yet: the twizzle, a one-foot turn. He usually worked with Vance Crowdell, trainer to the stars, but the man had some other arrangement tonight, so he'd been forced to train alone. Not that he minded. The crusty old trainer had already taught him so many new movements he needed to practice until he'd perfected those before learning any new ones.

And as he closed his eyes and allowed the music to take him into a new and wonderful world of glitter and glamor and thunderous applause, he saw himself as the first male Olympic figure skating gold medalist to come out of Britain in quite a long time.

* * *

Philo eyed the woman darkly. "I'm not asking, Madame Wu. I'm telling you. Take the package and hand it over as soon as you're told."

"But I can't," the proprietress of Xing Ming lamented in nasal tones. Her jet-black hair clearly came from a bottle and her horn-rimmed glasses were too large for her narrow face. She'd been running the small family restaurant for thirty years, one of the mainstays of London's Chinatown in the City of Westminster. "I have other matters tonight. I can't do package right now."

He thrust the package back into her hands. "Just take it

already. Lives depend on this," he added with a meaningful look. A look that said it was her own life that depended on it.

She rattled the package, her eyes unnaturally large behind the glasses. "What is it? Is it bomb?"

"No, is not bomb," he said, mimicking her accent. "It's just something very important." He leaned in. "Very important to Master Edwards."

A look of fear stole over her face, and she nodded quickly. "Yes, yes. Master Edwards. I will hand over package no problem. Hand over who?"

"You'll know her when you see her."< >

"Is woman?"

"Apparently."

Actually he didn't know himself. All he knew was that his contact had told him he would send his assistant, and she would be dressed in black. But since no one else knew about the package he wasn't too worried. He pointed a stubby finger at Madame Wu. "Just make sure she gets it, all right?"

She nodded, tucking the package beneath the counter. "Of course, Philo."

And as he stepped from the restaurant, the smell of Chinese food in his nostrils, he shook his head. Used to be that people like Madame Wu wouldn't dare contradict him, but that was before Master Edwards had fallen ill. The rumor that the old man was on the verge of death was spreading fast, and already his criminal empire was crumbling and his influence waning.

He crossed the busy street, bright neon lights announcing all manner of Asian food from every corner, and mounted the motorcycle he used to get around London in a hurry. And then he was off, narrowly missing the entry into the Chinese restaurant of a slender woman, all dressed in black.

It didn't take him long to race across town to his employer's house, in the heart of the East End. Master Edwards's house was located in a gated community, his own people providing protection, and Philo nodded to the guard as he passed. He'd hired him personally. A short drive up the hill led him to the house at the end of the street, which towered over all others. It used to belong to a famous actor in the sixties and was a sprawling mansion with fifty rooms, an underground pool, and cinema where Edwards and his cronies enjoyed watching gangster movies. Or rather, that's how it used to be.

He parked his bike in the garage and mounted the stairs, deftly making his way upstairs until he reached the landing and heard the telltale sounds of Master Edwards's snoring. Entering the bedroom, where the bedridden gang leader was laid up, he wasn't surprised to find him sound asleep. The moment he flicked on the light, the old man awoke with a start.

"Philo!" he muttered, blinking against the light. "Is that you?"

"It is, Master."

A look of annoyance crept into the man's eyes. "Why did you wake me?"

"Just to tell you that the package is being delivered as we speak."

The man's irritability dwindled. "Good," he said, settling back against the pillow. "Very good. Let's just hope the book works as advertised."

"I'm sure it will."

The old man licked his dry lips. "A lot depends on this, Philo. But then I probably don't need to remind you."

No, he didn't. He'd reminded him plenty of times since the chain of events had been set in motion a fortnight ago.

"There's only one small matter left to attend to," he said.

Master Edwards, whose eyes had drooped shut, opened them again. "Mh? What's that?"

"There's a witness," he said. "A young woman by the name of Henrietta McCabre. She's seen my face and might possibly become a nuisance."

"So?" snapped Master Edwards. "Just get it done, Philo. You don't need my permission to handle such a minor detail."

"No, Master," he said deferentially, though of course he did need the other's permission. In Master Edwards's world nothing ever happened without his approval, and most definitely not something of this importance.

"See to it that she's silenced, Philo. And make sure nobody sees you this time," the old man snapped, before closing his eyes once again. Soft snores soon sounded from the bed, and Philo bowed his head and retreated from the bedroom of his employer of twenty-five years. In this, the man's final days, he wasn't about to disappoint him. Not if he valued his own life. Henrietta McCabre, whoever she was, would not see her next birthday, he would make sure of that. And as he stalked over to his own room in the mansion, he sat down at the computer to begin an intense study of the life of Henrietta 'Harry' McCabre. This time, there would be no mistakes. And no witnesses.

Chapter Four

*B*right and early the next morning, Inspector Darian Watley frowned as he went over the evidence he'd gathered so far in the murder of Sir Geoffrey Buckley. He didn't have all that much to go on, he admitted ruefully. The crime scene had been squeaky clean, the safe revealing only Sir Buckley's prints and not even this McCabre woman's. The blow to the head he'd received had been the cause of death, all right, but of course there was no sign of the murder weapon. According to the coroner what they were looking for was a club of some kind. A heavy blunt object. Either that or someone possessing extraordinary strength.

Which was one of the reasons it was doubtful Henrietta McCabre was the culprit. She was of slight build and didn't possess the physical strength to kill a man with a single blow. No, whoever was responsible was probably a powerfully built male. That didn't mean she couldn't be an accomplice. His initial theory was that she'd somehow smuggled an associate into the shop, who'd done the dirty work and who'd absconded with the money and whatever other valuables Buckley kept locked up in his safe. At which point she'd called the police herself, so as not to draw suspicion to herself.

But then why had she left a million pounds in the store till?

He leaned forward in his chair and went over the CCTV footage his constable had collected. Going backward, it started with McCabre arriving at the store, then traced her movements back along the path she'd traveled until she disappeared from sight for half an hour. Coincidentally or not, she'd traveled to a part of London where no cameras could follow her. The theory was that she'd met someone there, for the cameras had picked her up again half an hour prior to her arrival at the underpass, coming from the store.

He quickly tracked other footage of cameras around the auspicious area, and to his surprise saw that a motorcycle arrived around the same time McCabre did and left again when she did. It couldn't be a coincidence.

She'd gone there to meet this mysterious motorcycle man.

He peered at the screen and started. "Well, I'll be damned," he muttered.

He quickly tapped a key and printed the image of Motorcycle Man. It wouldn't surprise him if he were implicated in the Buckley murder as well.

Of course, this presented him with a dilemma. Both McCabre and Motorcycle Man had an obvious alibi for the murder. And the most baffling thing of all: even though Buckley Antiques was covered by a camera from across the street, no one had entered or left the building around the time of the murder. He'd scrolled through the footage up until the time the police arrived, and the murderer was never seen leaving the premises.

Furthermore, there was no back entrance, nor a window through which the killer could have escaped. They'd checked with the inhabitants of the house sharing the back wall: there was no way to go from one to the other. They'd also checked the apartment above the store, but even there they hadn't found any manner of egress, not even along the roof of the building. It was, in other words, a real mystery how the killer had left.

He went over the footage captured around the time of the murder again. The only customer who'd been in the store was a young doctor, but she'd left at three forty-five. They'd interviewed her, and she hadn't seen anything out of the ordinary. And as Watley scrolled through the footage, he saw Buckley appearing at the door, bidding his final customer goodbye and even helping her carry her packages to her car, which was parked out in front. Then Buckley had retreated into the store, closed the door, and that had been the last time anyone had seen him alive. So whoever the murderer was, he or she had to have been inside, perhaps hiding? But they'd gone over the footage of the past twenty-four hours and everyone who'd entered the store had been seen leaving it at some point. No exception.

The only lead he had was the suspicious behavior of Henrietta McCabre and her meeting with Motorcycle Man. Those two could perhaps shed some light on the murder, as he was willing to bet they were both involved, as well as a third person, the one who'd actually perpetrated the murder.

All he had to do was find out why McCabre had gone to that meet.

And since he didn't like wasting time, he decided to pay her a visit right now. Rattle the cage a bit. And just when he was shrugging into his overcoat, his phone went, and he picked it up, barking, "Watley."

"Inspector Darian Watley?" a gruff voice sounded at the other end.

"Yes."

"I understand you're in charge of the Buckley murder investigation?"

"Who's asking?"

"Chief Whitehouse. Happy Bays Police Department."

Watley frowned. "Who? What?"

"Whitehouse. I'm chief of police in Happy Bays." There was a slight pause, then the man went on, "A small town on Long Island. The States."

Reluctantly he sat down again. "What can I do for you, Chief Whitehouse?" he asked, wondering what this was all about.

"I used to work for you guys at Scotland Yard about, oh, ten years ago? I worked under Thaddeus Yaffle at the time. Specialist Operations."

"Yaffle retired three years ago."

"I know. Good man, Thaddeus. You could always count on him to help you out in a pickle. My wife and I used to join him and his wife at your mother's dinner parties back in the day. And great parties they were."

Watley was starting to wonder if this Whitehouse would ever get to the point. "I wouldn't know. I never went to my mother's dinner parties."

"Met your dad once or twice. Great man, your dad. Great commissioner."

"Dad retired five years ago."

"Pity. He was always ready to help out a man in a pickle."

This obsession with pickles was starting to irk Darian. "And do you? Find yourself in a pickle, Chief Whitehouse?"

"Not me personally, but my niece does."

"And who is your niece?"

"Henrietta McCabre. My daughter tells me she's a suspect."

Watley raised his eyes to the ceiling. "Henrietta McCabre is your niece?"

"That's right. A very sweet-natured young woman. Absolutely incapable of murder. Or any other mischief for that matter. Which is why I'm calling."

If there was one thing Watley hated, it was outsiders butting into his investigation, and that included chiefs of police of small American towns. "Look here, Chief..." he began therefore, his tone not too friendly.

"I know what you're going to say," Whitehouse grumbled. "Butt out. I'd say exactly the same thing if I were in your position, Watley. But the fact of the matter is that I promised Harry I'd look after her. My sister and her husband died a couple of years ago, and her only other relatives are in Scotland and the States. And I hate to see Harry in a pickle like this."

"Well, that's entirely up to her now, isn't it? Nothing I can do about it," Watley returned. He was getting more and more annoyed. This Little Orphan Annie story might work on other people, but to him it reeked of manipulation.

"I'm going to ask you straight out, Watley. Is my niece a suspect?"

"I'm sorry, but as the investigation is still ongoing, I really don't see how I can disclose anything at this point, not even to a friend of my father."

"I see," said the man thoughtfully. "Then let me put it this way, Inspector. If anything were to happen to my niece, anything at all, I will personally come over there to make sure that the ones responsible will see justice served."

Watley gawked at the phone for a moment. Was this guy for real? "Are you threatening me?" he asked, his voice taking on a steely tone.

"Well, if the shoe fits…" riposted Whitehouse gruffly.

"If your niece finds herself in a pickle, I'd say she's the one responsible. Not me—not anyone else in the Yard—she and she alone!"

"So she is a suspect?"

"Of course she's a suspect!" he yelled. "She was meeting some guy at the time of the murder and refuses to tell me who he is and why they were meeting. Innocent people don't refuse to share this kind of information!"

Even before he'd finished talking, he knew he'd said too much. He was giving this man critical information from his investigation. This odd American who proclaimed to come after anyone who harmed his niece.

"I see," grunted Chief Whitehouse. "In that case, I'll have a word with my niece. I'm going to extract this piece of information from her, Watley, and then I'm going to share it with you. Together we're going to crack this case!"

Watley massaged his temple. "Please don't interfere with my investigation."

"Don't worry, buddy, I won't. I'm just going to talk to Harry, that's all. Get her to spill the beans." He barked a curt laugh. "I like this, Watley. I like this intercontinental cooperation we've got going here. Just like old times."

"Please. Sir. I really don't need your help," he said curtly.

"You don't have to thank me, Watley. Just doing what needs to be done!"

"I'm not thanking you, and nothing needs to be done!" he cried.

"How would you feel," the other man rumbled, "if you had an orphaned niece, living all alone in a big city, her boss murdered, and no one around to help her? No family, no job, no future prospects, hounded by the cops..."

"Hey! I'm not hounding your niece!"

"I'm going to get to the bottom of this and then I'll get back to you, Watley. Can I call you Darian?"

"No, you may not!"

"Great. Just call me Curtis. Much appreciated, Darian. And say hi to your mom and dad, will you? My wife still raves about those dinner parties."

"Wait—you can't do this!"

"Good day to you, too," the chief growled, and promptly disconnected.

Watley stared at his phone. What the hell had just happened? But then he knew exactly what had happened. For some nebulous reason, he'd just been coerced into an intercontinental investigation into the Buckley murder.

"God," he groaned as he raked a hand through his dark mane. Just what he needed right now. Some gung-ho small-town cop to add to his problems.

He quickly rose again and swept from his office. Before her

uncle started throwing his weight about, he was going to make Henrietta McCabre talk, and he was going to do it now. He didn't care that she was an orphan, she was going to tell him exactly what had happened under that underpass.

Chapter Five

*T*en minutes later, he was chauffeuring his car through London morning traffic, en route to Valentine Street, where Henrietta McCabre was apparently housed. When he arrived, and finally managed to find a parking space, he strode up to the house and pressed his finger on the bell. He hadn't told her he was coming, lest she made up some excuse. When he heard her melodious voice inquire about his identity, he barked, "Inspector Watley, Miss McCabre. I have a few more questions for you if you don't mind."

Whitehouse might call this hounding. He called it proper police work.

After a brief pause, she buzzed him in, and he found himself in the narrow hallway of a clean-looking house. She called from upstairs, "Second floor, Inspector!" and he grunted and started to make his way up the stairs.

When he arrived on the landing, he saw that she'd changed into something less sodding wet than the day before. A pair of pink linen pants and bright yellow linen shirt. It became her. She was an attractive young woman, he had to admit, but then he'd noticed that already when he'd interviewed her before.

With her short bob of blond hair, fair complexion and lithe frame she looked anywhere between eighteen and twenty-five, though he knew from her file she was, in fact, twenty-three.

Her nose tilted up at the tip, and her eyes were large and of a remarkable golden hue. All in all, she looked entirely too pretty to be a suspect, and he really couldn't imagine she was involved in anything as nasty as murder. But then if his years in the Yard had taught him anything it was that looks could be deceiving. For all he knew here stood a cold-blooded accomplice to murder.

"Pancake, Mr. Watley?"

"Inspector Watley. No, thank you, Miss McCabre. I never eat when I'm on duty."

"Suit yourself," she said, inviting him in. "I just baked up an entire batch. Didn't know what else to do, to be honest. Being out of a job and all."

The smell of freshly baked pancakes did indeed waft invitingly from the small space. Small but cozy, he thought as he briefly inspected the living room with TV nook and kitchen nook. It was airy and light, and the color scheme was the same as her clothes: lots of bright pinks and yellows.

"I just got a call from your uncle," he said, opening the proceedings.

She halted in her tracks. "My uncle?"

"Chief Whitehouse of the Happy Bays Police Department. He seems to be under the impression you need protecting from the big bad policeman." He grimaced and pointed at himself. "From me, in fact."

Her face reddened slightly. It became her well, he thought, before instantly stomping on this thought. She was a suspect. Nothing more.

"Oh, I'm so sorry about that," she murmured, looking mortified.

"I can't imagine that you are. I mean, you must have told him, right? You must have called him last night and asked him to put in a word on your behalf."

She frowned. "No, I didn't. Well, not directly. I mean, I called my cousin. But all I asked her was if her dad knew someone at Scotland Yard."

"And now he does know someone at Scotland Yard. And you do, too."

"I meant someone I could talk to about…" she gestured ineffectually. "…stuff."

He pulled out a chair in the kitchen nook and took a seat. "Let's cut to the chase, Miss McCabre."

"Harry, please."

"Where are you on your alibi, Miss McCabre?"

She gulped slightly. "My… alibi?"

"Yes. Remember I asked you where you were yesterday between three and four and you failed to inform me? Now perhaps, after mulling it over, you might be able to elucidate me? Or did your uncle advise you not to disclose this information?"

A blush mantled her cheeks. "My uncle said no such thing. I haven't spoken to him in ages."

"Oh, that's right. You spoke to your cousin," he said skeptically.

"Look, I could tell you where I was," she said with a shake of the head as she flipped another pancake onto a plate, "but I'd rather not, you see?"

"No, I don't see. This is very serious matter, Miss McCabre."

She smiled. "Why don't you just call me Harry? All my friends do."

"I'm not your friend, Miss McCabre. I'm a Scotland Yard inspector investigating a murder," he insisted. "And what I'm most interested in right now is ascertaining where you were yesterday between three and four. In other words, around the time your employer was brutally murdered."

She sighed. "Look, you'll probably think this is all very silly, but if I tell you where I was... There're other people involved, see? I mean, if it were just me, I'd tell you where I was in a heartbeat, but it's not just me, is it?"

"Who else is involved?" he asked, following her movements with an interested eye. Those pancakes really did smell quite delicious.

"I can't tell you! That's just the point! Look," she said, taking a seat at the table across from him, "Mr. Buckley did some of his deals, erm, well, under the table. I mean, they weren't exactly shady deals or anything like that, it's just that his clients preferred... discretion, I guess you could say."

"I'm well aware that Buckley was one of the more prominent fences in the world of antiques, Miss McCabre," he said, eliciting a gasp of surprise from her. "Which is probably the reason he was murdered. In those circles, a life is often worth a great deal less than some nice painting or fancy old cupboard."

She deftly picked up a pancake and started slathering it with butter and jam. "Well, if you know about Buckley's business, then you must know that he used me to, well, deliver some of his packages to some of his clients."

"So what package were you delivering to which client yesterday?"

She threw up her hands, then licked some jam from her wrist. "I can't tell you, can I? Otherwise I'd be implicating my client, see?"

He gave her a slight smile, like a cat about to devour a mouse. "If you don't tell me it implicates you. It turns you into one of our prime suspects in this murder, and I may very well have to take you in for further questioning."

Her eyes went wide, and he was surprised to find how expressive they were. Her every emotion was very clearly reflected in those golden orbs.

"You mean arrest me? What would you go and do a silly thing like that for?!"

"Because you're refusing to tell me what I need to know!" he shot back, his smile gone. "Look, I don't know what your uncle advised you, but—"

"My uncle didn't advise me anything! Like I said, I talked to my cousin."

"Is she also a cop? Is she the one who told you to keep secrets from the police? Is that how they do things in the States?"

She eyed him huffily. "My cousin, if you must know, works as a mortician's assistant, gun store clerk and tea room waitress. Though at one time she did want to become a cop and even went to police academy. But that's neither here nor there. What matters is—"

"What matters is that you tell me what I want to know," he cut in, "or I'm going to have to arrest you on suspicion of conspiracy to commit murder."

There was a momentary silence as they gazed at each other, the tension palpable. Then she simply said, "Very well. I'll tell you what I know, which isn't much, mind you."

"I'll be the judge of that, Miss McCabre."

"Harry," she corrected him.

"Just tell me already, will you?!" he yelled.

She rolled her eyes. "Oh, all right! But if he's cross with me I'll tell him you made me tell on him! And if he tells me I'm a tattletale I'll tell him it's all your fault!"

"Miss McCabre!"

"Harry!"

"Talk!"

She stared at him, biting her lip. "Actually… I don't know his name."

About Nic

Nic Saint is the pen name for writing couple Nick and Nicole Saint. They've penned 40+ novels in the romance, cat sleuth, middle grade, suspense, comedy and cozy mystery genres. Nicole has a background in accounting and Nick in political science and before being struck by the writing bug the Saints worked odd jobs around the world (including massage therapist in Mexico, gardener in Italy, restaurant manager in India, and Berlitz teacher in Belgium).

When they're not writing they enjoy Christmas-themed Hallmark movies (whether it's Christmas or not), all manner of pastry, comic books, a daily dose of yoga (to limber up those limbs), and spoiling their big red tomcat Tommy.

Get Nic Saint's books FOR FREE

Sign up for the no-spam newsletter and get FREE reads and lots more exclusive content: nicsaint.com/newsletter.

Also by Nic Saint

The Mysteries of Bell & Whitehouse

One Spoonful of Trouble
Two Scoops of Murder
Three Shots of Disaster
A Twist of Wraith
A Touch of Ghost
A Clash of Spooks
The Stuffing of Nightmares
A Breath of Dead Air

Ghosts of London

Between a Ghost and a Spooky Place

Witchy Fingers

Witchy Trouble

Other Books

When in Bruges
Once Upon a Spy
The Whiskered Spy

83795966R00123

Made in the USA
Middletown, DE
15 August 2018